Abandon

Also from Rachel Van Dyken

Liars, Inc.
Dirty Exes

The Players Game Series
Fraternize
Infraction
MVP

The Consequence Series
The Consequence of Loving Colton
The Consequence of Revenge
The Consequence of Seduction
The Consequence of Rejection

The Wingmen Inc. Series
The Matchmaker's Playbook
The Matchmaker's Replacement

Curious Liaisons Series
Cheater
Cheater's Regret

The Bet Series
The Bet
The Wager
The Dare

The Ruin Series
Ruin
Toxic
Fearless
Shame

The Eagle Elite Series
Elite
Elect

Enamor
Entice
Elicit
Bang Bang
Enforce
Ember
Elude
Empire
Enrage
Eulogy
Envy

The Seaside Series
Tear
Pull
Shatter
Forever
Fall
Eternal
Strung
Capture

The Renwick House Series
The Ugly Duckling Debutante
The Seduction of Sebastian St. James
An Unlikely Alliance
The Redemption of Lord Rawlings
The Devil Duke Takes a Bride

The London Fairy Tales Series
Upon a Midnight Dream
Whispered Music
The Wolf's Pursuit
When Ash Falls

The Seasons of Paleo Series
Savage Winter
Feral Spring

Abandon

A Seaside Pictures Novella

By Rachel Van Dyken

1001 Dark Nights

EVIL EYE
CONCEPTS

Abandon
A Seaside Pictures Novella
By Rachel Van Dyken

1001 Dark Nights

Copyright 2019 Rachel Van Dyken
ISBN: 978-1-970077-26-1

Foreword: Copyright 2014 M. J. Rose

Published by Evil Eye Concepts, Incorporated

Acknowledgments from the Author

This is always the hardest part for an author. I'm so incredibly grateful to God that I get to wake up every single day and do something that I love, that I'm able to write stories that hopefully give people a much needed escape from the stress of life! Thank you so much, Liz Berry, for giving me the privilege to write stories for 1001 Dark Nights. To the whole 1001 Dark Nights team, I remember thinking that it would be a dream to work with you guys and now I'm living that dream! A special thank you to my beta readers, editors, and assistants who helped me whip this one out a bit faster than the other ones. Thank you, Nina, for being patient with my schedule every time I tell you my deadlines. Bloggers, readers, thank you so much for reading, reviewing, and sharing. I truly wouldn't have a job without you guys. Your love for books is contagious. And last but not least thanks to the husband for taking little man swimming while I stayed up late and tried to finish the book. Oh, and I'm sorry about all the pizza! If you want to follow my writing journey visit my website www.rachelvandykenauthor.com or join my ridiculously awesome reader group Rachels New Rockin Readers via Facebook, you can also find me on Insta/Twitter @RachVD, hugs, and cheers to another HEA!

One Thousand and One Dark Nights

Once upon a time, in the future...

*I was a student fascinated with stories and learning.
I studied philosophy, poetry, history, the occult, and
the art and science of love and magic. I had a vast
library at my father's home and collected thousands
of volumes of fantastic tales.*

*I learned all about ancient races and bygone
times. About myths and legends and dreams of all
people through the millennium. And the more I read
the stronger my imagination grew until I discovered
that I was able to travel into the stories... to actually
become part of them.*

*I wish I could say that I listened to my teacher
and respected my gift, as I ought to have. If I had, I
would not be telling you this tale now.
But I was foolhardy and confused, showing off
with bravery.*

*One afternoon, curious about the myth of the
Arabian Nights, I traveled back to ancient Persia to
see for myself if it was true that every day Shahryar
(Persian: شهریار, "king") married a new virgin, and then
sent yesterday's wife to be beheaded. It was written
and I had read, that by the time he met Scheherazade,
the vizier's daughter, he'd killed one thousand
women.*

*Something went wrong with my efforts. I arrived
in the midst of the story and somehow exchanged
places with Scheherazade – a phenomena that had
never occurred before and that still to this day, I
cannot explain.*

*Now I am trapped in that ancient past. I have
taken on Scheherazade's life and the only way I can
protect myself and stay alive is to do what she did to
protect herself and stay alive.*

*Every night the King calls for me and listens as I spin tales.
And when the evening ends and dawn breaks, I stop at a
point that leaves him breathless and yearning for more.
And so the King spares my life for one more day, so that
he might hear the rest of my dark tale.*

*As soon as I finish a story... I begin a new
one... like the one that you, dear reader, have before
you now.*

Chapter One

Ty

"You ready?" I gripped my drumsticks tightly in my right hand as the screaming from the crowd pierced my ears, causing an onslaught of adrenaline to pulse beneath my skin.

Drew, one of the leading frontmen for our band, Adrenaline, rolled his eyes and shot me a middle finger. Then he straight-up tugged his leather pants down below his hips to show off his legendary V.

We get it, bro, you've got an eight-pack where there's usually only six.

With a flourish, I pulled off my simple white tee and shrugged. "What? Two can play that game."

"Seriously, guys?" Will gave me a shove. "They already gave us shit last time about you two comparing dicks. It's the Grammys, not the Super Bowl. We have to be clothed."

I eyed him up and down. "Question. Was it your plan to go out there looking like the dad of the group, or was it just a happy accident?" He was in skinny jeans and a simple vintage tee and wore his typical thick black glasses that somehow still got him action from his wife, actress Angelica Greene. It was confusing when Will got action and I didn't.

Not that I wasn't getting any.

I inwardly smirked. I was dating one of our background dancers, while at the same time hooking up with one of Zane's—both of which were performing with us tonight. Hey, it wasn't like I planned for them to ever meet! And before you get your panties in a twist and start calling me a whore while chanting things like *"I pray your dick falls off,"* let me explain.

I have a solid reason for dating both women.

You ready for it?

The truth bomb of the century?

I don't actually have a heart. You see, a long time ago in a land where my innocence thrived—you know, before the mistakes with the drugs, alcohol, and the time I carried a live chicken on stage and kissed it—I was in love.

Real love.

Not the kind where you say it just because you want to have sex with someone so badly, you're willing to sell your soul to the devil. Twice.

Real, honest to God love.

Her name? Abigail.

Her current status? Breaker of souls and spawn of Satan.

I had been twenty-three to her twenty-one when we went on tour together. And, well, I fell in love with the way she strummed her guitar. About the same time, she fell in love with the way I banged on the drums like a complete idiot.

We were together until our schedules got in the way. One day, she just told me she was through. That she couldn't take it anymore.

And then, she walked away.

Of course, she had no way of knowing that I was gripping a diamond ring in my right hand, or that my left hand was sweating profusely and dying a slow death from the thorns in the single white rose I carried. She wouldn't know because she never looked back.

"Let's go!" Trevor shouted behind me, completely ruining my stroll down memory lane, along with storytime. He massaged my shoulders then kicked me in the ass with his booted foot.

It wasn't like my story was that interesting anyway. Kind of depressing, if you asked me—or anyone else who'd had to witness my three-year drug-induced spiral.

Something not worth mentioning, considering I was one hundred percent clean of all mind-altering drugs, except for random shots of whiskey. Just the smell of gin and tonic made me want to hurl.

The point: I was dating two girls.

And I had pretty damn good reasons for dating two.

So I didn't accidentally get too attached to one.

Brilliant, right?

The commercial break ended, and we were waved onstage. The screams grew even louder. I grinned as I went behind my drum set and started our countdown.

"One, two. One, two, three, four." I hit my sticks and filled the auditorium with my beat while Drew started crooning our newest breakup song into the microphone. Trevor played guitar in front of me, while Will flanked him on the right. Suddenly, everything felt perfect in my world again.

Because of the music.

The background dancers were supposed to move into focus once we hit the second verse, but for now, it was just us and the music.

I closed my eyes as we hit the chorus, playing my heart out and singing harmony into the microphone.

Three minutes.

It was three minutes of perfection.

When I opened my eyes as Drew sang the last part of the chorus, I noticed something out of the corner of my eye.

Or should I say some*ones*?

The women I was dating. Both dancers were going at it when they should have been doing the choreographed routine.

Well, shit.

They were shouting at each other and pointing at me while I tried to keep up with the second verse and the chorus. One tripped the other as they stumbled towards me. And…double shit. Smile, just smile!

Finish the song, finish the song, I thought while Drew seemed to sing forever.

All it took was one slap and a punch, and one of the girls went sailing into my cymbals, causing them to topple over onto my half-naked body. The woman followed, and the other jumped on top of both of us, screaming. Thankfully, the music was too loud to hear all the horrible things she called both me and the other background dancer.

I had been raised a gentleman, so I couldn't exactly fight back, even if they railed on me. My grandma would murder me. God bless her soul.

I waited, hoping they'd get distracted by the crowd of celebrities instead of focusing on the horror on my face.

They didn't.

And suddenly, the whole a-woman-scorned-is-a-scary-thing saying entered my mind as two pairs of demonic eyes glared back at me.

I was going to die today.

Farewell, world.

It'd been a fun ride, but—

"Oomph. Son of—" They shoved me onto my back, my drumsticks flying, the drums falling on top of them as they slapped.

All the slapping.

My face.

My naked torso.

And yes, good friends, sadly my dick. It was persecuted in a way that should never be spoken of again. Ever. Ever again.

"You lying son of a bitch!" girl one yelled.

"I can't believe I fell for it!" The roommate kneed me in the balls, likely rendering me unable to father offspring.

The crowd went even wilder as security pulled both women off of me and took them backstage.

I knew we were live.

I knew people were staring.

So I did what I always did when I had all eyes on me. Even though my dick had a pulse, I jumped into the air with both drumsticks and shouted, "Breakups suck!"

The cheer was deafening.

The looks on my bandmates' faces, however, were damning.

Well, fuck.

Chapter Two

Ty

1 month later...

"This town is where sadness goes to thrive, and happiness goes to die," I mumbled under my breath as yet another rainstorm from hell pounded onto my already wet black beanie and long-sleeve shirt.

I lived in Los Angeles for a reason.

Sunshine.

Seaside, Oregon, it seemed was allergic to all things sun-related. Oh, they tried to sell you on how nice the white sand beaches were or how cool the small-ass aquarium could be on a rainy day. But the truth about Seaside?

It was only nice when it was nice outside, and it hadn't been nice for thirty solid days. In fact, I was convinced that I was coming down with seasonal affective disorder from all the clouds.

At this rate, I would have to take up tanning and vitamin D supplements to make sure I didn't spiral.

Darkness seemed to trigger me.

And a triggered Ty Cuban was not a good thing.

It made me feel like crawling out of my skin. I couldn't even hike, longboard, or really do anything in these conditions—not with all the flash floods. And to make matters worse?

Today was the first day of the Hollywood Music Camp. And no, before you ask, I did not come up with that ridiculous name. Slap *Hollywood* on something and people just shelled out a shit-ton of money, didn't they?

Hollywood Music Camp—or HMC as I'd decided to call it—was a sister camp to a famous drama camp in New York. With my band's help, and that of my other friend's group, AD2, and Zane "Saint" Andrews—the guy who never wore shirts or pants for that matter in public—we'd helped to fund a second location of the camp focused on music.

At the time, I'd thought I was just writing a check and doing a sponsored post on Instagram.

Wrong.

Especially after that…ahem, minor incident at the Grammys, my bandmates had come up with a better plan.

Teaching.

Yeah, just call me Mr. Cuban and find me a sweater vest because who else did you want teaching your easily influenced middle-schoolers but a rock star who got attacked on national television?

Right.

The rain seemed to increase as I made my way toward the beach where the company had set up several tents with heaters under them. It was supposed to take place outside, just like the rain was supposed to let up days ago.

I felt soggy and irritated as I made my way toward the different white tents. At least a hundred kids ranging from the ages of ten to eighteen scrambled around snack tables like piranhas.

I'd be lucky if I got a Dorito crumb at this rate. Not that I was willing to fight the little man in the *Wakanda Forever* shirt for a taste. I figured he'd probably just scream "*Wakanda*" and throat-punch me. Not worth it.

Even if it was the cool ranch Doritos—the only kind worth getting in a fight for.

I looked to the right. There was a small stage set up with every single instrument you could imagine, and near the stage, a sign that said *blankets* with an arrow pointing down. Huh, at least we wouldn't freeze to death.

The tents circled around a giant bonfire where a few members of AD2 were obviously trying to see how close they could get without getting singed. Either that, or Demetri Daniels was attempting to make the fire bigger and was in over his head.

I made my way over just in time for Alec Daniels, the other member of the duo AD2, to look up and give me a shit-eating grin.

I knew that expression.

It was the exact same one every bandmate had given me when it was announced that I would be volunteering this summer instead of Trevor.

Bastard was planning his wedding, so it only made sense that I would help instead. The best part? Trevor freaking lived here. I was the one who had to pack all my shit and move for a few months.

At least he was letting me stay with him. That was my first thought when I arrived at his nice beach house.

But within five seconds of greeting him, I'd been attacked by ice cream hands, had nearly chipped a tooth on a Lego, and witnessed the screams of a little girl who thought she was dying because she lost a tooth.

I was single for a reason.

"Hey, man." Alec pulled me in for a hug. "Happy you made it."

"Yes," I deadpanned. "Overjoyed."

He rolled his eyes. "They're just kids."

"That's like saying a bull is just a steak."

"Or a chicken is safe," Demetri piped up from his spot near the fire. He had blond hair and light eyes, and the women basically swooned every time he opened his mouth. Alec was all dark tattoos, dark hair, and light eyes, which just made him look like the bad boy of the group when that title actually went to the one poking the fire with the stick.

"Need some help building the fire, Dem?" I grinned and circled the pitiful thing. "Or do you have the situation handled?"

"He has nothing handled," Alec mumbled under his breath as a spark flew out and nearly rendered him dickless.

At least I had friends with me and I wasn't teaching on my own. A few other musicians were helping out. I'd toured with all of them at least once, which made it feel a lot less like summer camp.

The rain finally started to let up as the sun pushed through the clouds. Huh, maybe it wouldn't be so bad, after all.

Maybe this would be more vacation and less work.

I opened my mouth to say something stupid to the universe like,

"*Wow, this isn't so bad, after all,*" only I was interrupted. By something familiar.

Something that made my hair stand on end, and my testicles run for cover. A sperm may have even lost its life because of that voice.

Abigail.

Freaking Abigail Von.

"No!" she yelled. "Nope! Not doing it. You're all liars from the pit of hell. How could you?"

I turned just in time to see Zane Andrews shoving her in my direction with a cocky grin on his face. No shirt, and pants that looked as if they'd been painted on his tatted-up body. His nose ring straight-up winked at me, while his smile grew as if he'd planned this deception all along.

"Ah, Satan." I crossed my arms and glared at her. "How's hell these days? Still hot?"

Her blue eyes narrowed. "Searing. And far enough away from you and your whores that it's almost like Christmas every single day!"

"Aw, I'll be sure to send a ham for the celebration." I eyed her up and down. "Maybe more protein, less carbs. Yeah, Abs?"

"Son of a—" She lunged at me, and Zane just barely pulled her back while I nearly stumbled into the minuscule fire that Demetri had likely strained a brain cell trying to build.

"Everything okay over here?" Trevor, my bandmate, roommate, the one engaged to the nanny—long story, don't ask—jogged over and looked between us. He paled. "Don't you two have a restraining order?"

"Only in my heart." I patted my chest and blew her a kiss while she tried lunging at me again.

"No offense, Abby"—Trevor held up his hands—"but I didn't see you on the staff sheet."

"Oh, I added her last minute." Zane finally spoke. "We were down one person."

"Who isn't coming?" I asked as sweat started to trickle down my back.

"Will." Zane grinned. Our lead singer was supposed to at least make an appearance. "He's sick." Zane chose that moment to cough, as if proving Will's sickness by example.

"I call bullshit," I said through clenched teeth. "He's never sick!"

"His wife's pregnant." Zane shrugged. "He's her husband, so he's having sympathy sickness. Look it up, it's a thing."

"It actually is a thing," Alec said, not so helpfully.

I shot him a look. "Could you just not right now?"

Zane shrugged. "Either way, it's not like you guys have to breathe the same air or anything. You'll be with students for six hours a day. Just try not to murder each other in front of any little kid who's going to witness what happens and post to their Snapchat, and you should be fine!"

"As always…" I couldn't take my eyes off her. "So helpful."

"Oh, trust me"—Abby looked up at me with hatred—"I'll stay far, far away."

Something in my chest cracked as I whispered, "She's good at that. Staying far away then walking away altogether." I turned around and left.

Chapter Three

Abigail

How did one explain the complicated mess that was Ty Cuban? I hated how good he looked. All ripped in the right places in tight jeans and his ever-present white V-neck that showed off the tattoos I remembered running my hands over countless times.

He was a menace to society.

And I'd fought with him more than I cared to admit. The problem between us had always been our explosive tempers. Well, that and the fact that we were so ridiculously young when we first hooked up. We'd joked about doing a Google search on sexual positions that wouldn't get a girl pregnant.

Yeah, we were that stupid.

He was my first everything.

My first love.

My first kiss.

My first sexual experience.

And, sadly, if I dug into the darkest crevice of my heart where I shoved every memory of Ty Cuban, he'd been my best friend.

At least that's how it had been before everything went down in fiery glory. Because Ty loved attention, and he loved being the center of it at all times. Which meant I had often been ignored and shoved out of the way when there were fans around. His rule was that our relationship was never allowed to come to the point where we isolated ourselves from the world or from our jobs. I had been a solo artist on my very first world tour, and he was a rock god who had websites dedicated to his smirk.

Seriously, I'd been on the receiving end of that smirk more times than I'd like to admit. And several times, it felt like my clothes were just melting off my body. Either that, or it made me so hot I wished for a sudden firestorm so I could be naked.

I watched him walk away and ignored the very real pain that sliced through my chest at seeing him again. At being set up and forced to work alongside someone who truly didn't play well with others.

When Zane called, I'd jumped at the chance to do this, only because I'd just gone through a horrible breakup with my boyfriend of three years. I'd dumped his clothes in the front yard of my Malibu beach house and set them on fire. Then again, I *had* warned him what would happen if I caught him cheating.

Again.

Lucky me, he was just stupid enough to do it in our house.

Our bed, specifically. I had gotten home early from the studio, bottle of wine in hand, ready to celebrate finishing my fifth album when I heard giggling.

I hated girls who giggled.

Give me a good throaty laugh any day of the week. A giggle was just stupidity at its finest.

Then again, Harrison liked that sort of thing. He'd always complained that I was too aggressive. Not soft enough.

Well, the giggler was soft all right. With giant boobs, hair, lips… And, yeah, maybe I had been a bit jealous that she was everything I wasn't.

Where I had a full sleeve of tattoos, she had perfect, tan skin. I had long, golden-brown hair that had a fade down the right side, multiple piercings in my ears, and a nose ring.

She was…pure.

Damn it.

I kicked some sand and sat down in a huff, holding my knees to my chest, probably making a scene and really not caring.

"You lied," I said through clenched teeth when Zane plopped down next to me. We'd been friends for years—a decade at least. I'd toured with him twice, and he was one of the nicest people I'd ever met. But I'd never seen him as anything but that. A friend.

And now that he was married, it just seemed weird talking to him about my past, my relationship problems. Everything.

"I may have…omitted." He shrugged. His friggin' eight-pack flexed as he leaned back on his forearms and grinned up at me. "You know you still like him. That little flame you've been holding must be getting hot, hmm?"

I flipped him off just in time for Drew, one of the final members of Ty's band Adrenaline, to show up and sit on the other side of me. If Zane had an evil, just-as-hot—or maybe even hotter—twin, it would be Drew.

"Ah, prodigal, you're back." I slugged him in the rock-hard shoulder, earning a little wink from him as he pulled out a guitar pick and started sucking on it like it was a cigarette.

Out of all the guys, he was the one I worried about the most.

He was the one Ty had always said he was afraid would go off the deep end.

Part of me wondered if I was the reason Ty had turned into the manwhore of the century and had been caught with drugs twice.

Then again, we'd both done things.

The hurt was shared.

And when comparing broken hearts, did it really matter how big the shards were? Broken was broken.

I swallowed past the lump in my throat.

"This have anything to do with the fact that Ty just cussed me out in front of a seven-year-old kid that told him he should wash his mouth out with soap?"

I burst out laughing. "Tell me you got that on Snapchat."

"Damn hands weren't fast enough." He laughed. "But, to his credit, Ty did apologize, then took a picture with the kid and told him to just say no to drugs." Drew made little air quotes, while Zane and I snorted. "What?"

"What do you mean…what?" I elbowed him. "Like Ty should be telling anyone to stay off drugs—"

"He's clean," Drew interrupted. "For the record, we all are. We take weekly drug tests. Not that it's any of your business."

I looked away.

"It's okay," Zane said softly. "You haven't been around much. People change. They do this thing called adulting. Don't ask me the actual definition though, because I'm still on the struggle bus. Thankfully, I have a gorgeous glasses-wearing girl to go home to, and she helps me with the big words and makes sure I know how to fix the dishwasher."

"Broke again?" Drew snickered.

"F. U." Zane censored himself as a kid ran by us. "I'm going to win."

Drew nodded to me. "Now that he's domesticated, he thinks he can fix everything. Just don't trigger him and ask about the garage."

"Zane?" I turned to him. "You wanna tell me something?"

"Yeah." He glared over my head at Drew. "Drew's sad because he's single and he hasn't slept with anyone in two years. Damn." He put his hand on his torso. "Feels so good to get that off my chest."

"Hey, question." Drew raised his hand. "Weren't you a virgin for like twenty-two years?"

"Break it up." Alec's voice interrupted us. "We're about ready to get started. Just remember, you're here to inspire, take selfies, teach the kids how to play guitar, and that's it. And now we owe them a kick-ass opening concert!"

"Yayyyy…" Drew said in a sing-song voice. "By the way, I'm so glad most of us get to leave after a few weeks. How long you staying?"

"Me?" He was asking me. I wanted to lie, but I'd packed up enough clothes to stay longer than a month or two, and I'd already looked at property because maybe all the celebs in the area had a point. They all had a house here to get away from everything.

At least Ty wasn't staying.

Maybe I truly would be getting away from everything.

But why did that make me sad?

"Up you go." Alec helped me to my feet. "You're on background vocals and bass, that all right?"

"As long as I'm far, far, away from Ty," I grumbled.

"That's the stage." Alec pointed to a small stage near the front of the white tents where the kids were already cheering and pulling out their blankets.

I would be close enough to Ty to hear his breathing when the music wasn't playing. Part of me would do a dance on his corpse if he stopped taking in those breaths.

The other part?

It would die right along with him.

Why was love so difficult?

Chapter Four

Ty

It was going to be a long day.

Avoiding her would be impossible, and I was turning into the exact kind of creeper every woman who dumped me always said I would be. I guess, not really a creeper.

I was just watching her play guitar.

Watching her hands move.

Remembering the days we used to write music together and lay out in the sun, our guitars between us, holding hands.

Son of a bitch. Minutes in her presence and I was already traveling down memory lane.

I hated that lane.

Blew it up ten years ago and put a giant *Do Not Enter* sign in front of it.

Nothing good ever came from regretting something you couldn't change, and there wasn't anything I could change about what had happened.

The intro stopped as Alec put his hands in the air to hush the excited kids, all of them were so…happy.

I frowned.

Music used to make me feel that way.

It still did.

But it'd lost a lot of its spark the minute my muse walked out of my life.

I refused to tell her that it had made me spiral. That she'd had that much control over my life, over me.

"Hey, everyone! I'm Alec Daniels, and this, as you all know, is my brother, Demetri. We'll be in charge of the music summer program this year and can't wait to help you guys with your music!"

Cheers ensued.

I shot a glare to Abby about the same time she flipped me off behind her back.

Old habits.

Perfect.

Drew gave me a cut-it-out look from his spot on the right. He was the only bandmate that could keep me in line since Will was apparently *pregnant*, and Trevor was being a father to his kids.

Grumble, grumble, grumble. That's what I felt like.

Zane joined everyone on stage—this time clothed, thank God— and grabbed a mic from Demetri. "And you guys know me, the ever-amazing Zane 'Saint' Andrews."

Screams this time.

Of course, he'd just graced the cover of *People*.

Bastard was good-looking, I'd give him that.

"We're really happy to be here. We have some incredible musicians flying in over the next two months, and a few surprises up our sleeves. Don't forget that open mic night is every Wednesday, and that every time you perform, you're entered to win backstage passes for our next tour starting this winter. Everyone you see here on this stage will be touring and performing, so it's going to be a great show—"

My mind went blank.

I stared.

And stared harder.

Gaped over at Drew, who was looking anywhere but at me while the guys all high-fived each other up front.

And then my gaze moved to Abby, who had gone completely ashen as if someone had forgotten to tell both of us.

My mind reeled. She did just finish her last album…

We were doing a second tour of our latest release since we had so many sold-out venues.

AD2 was always supposed to come with Zane and us.

What. The. Hell?

I stood, my drumsticks hanging by my sides, and fucking walked off that stage like a petulant child. Because my bandmates were supposed to be my family.

And family didn't do that.

Not when they knew your past.

Not when they knew how long it'd taken you to get over the shit you went through.

"Ty!" Drew's voice.

"What?" I didn't turn around, just kept walking. At least the rain had stopped.

And just like that, my universe shook, and rain started to pour.

I looked up at the sky. "Really? *Really?*"

"Hold up." Drew grabbed my shoulder. "I was waiting to tell you. We all were."

"Waiting to tell me that the spawn of Satan would be touring with us for three months? When would be a good time?"

Drew's face hardened. "Oh, I don't know, maybe before you made us look like complete dicks at the Grammys. No, no, that would have been too difficult since you were busy screwing two girls at the same time while eyeing the groupies. Hmmm, I could have done it after that when you packed your shit and moved to Seaside without saying anything to us and making us think you were dead, only to call us a week later and threaten to quit the band. No, that wouldn't have been good either because everyone's so terrified of setting you off and sending you—" He gulped. "I know how it is. You know I do. But it's like walking on eggshells around you lately. And you can blame Abby all you want, but this is on you. You aren't happy, and you haven't been happy for a while. You screw anything that walks, refuse to take any of this seriously, and act like you're still twenty-one!"

"I'm not that old!" I said defensively.

"Stop fixating on the shit that doesn't matter. She's good for ticket sales—not that we need it. And we're at the same record company, all right? It made sense. We voted, and since you screwed up, you didn't get a vote. I'm sorry you're going through shit." He kicked the sand. "But grow the hell up, all right?"

"This coming from the guy that refuses to even talk about anything personal," I snapped.

He ground his teeth. "It's different."

"Says the one I used to get high with," I snapped. "Yeah, sure, it's totally different. Scars may look different, but they feel the same."

He sighed and ran his hands through his hair. "Look, we'll compromise, okay? How about I talk to the guys, and you stay and teach in Trevor's studio, so you don't have to see her every day?"

My ears perked up. "Wait, you would do that?"

"On one condition." I didn't like the way he grinned at me. "You have to promise me that if I can convince them to let you bow out for the summer and teach at the studio, that you compose three new songs."

I rolled my eyes. "I can do that in my sleep."

"I wasn't finished."

Shit.

"Three new songs. *And* you have to spend at least one night a week with Abby."

"You want me to spend the night?" I choked. "In a bed?"

"See, this is why you got mauled at the Grammys. No, you dick, I want you to spend a night, a few hours, trying to fix things so it's not a shit show when we all go on tour."

I opened my mouth to argue, then did the math. "Three hours tops."

"Fine."

"Good." I snorted.

"Fantastic." He let out a grunt. "Now, get your ass back to the tent, paste a smile on that ugly face of yours, and play the set. When you're done, I'll talk to the guys and get a schedule from Trevor. He's been stressed out over all the students he's been getting this summer anyway, and a few of them are doing the summer camp along with private lessons. It would be good to have you there, helping."

The tightness in my chest dissipated a bit. "Yeah. Plus, I like Trevor more than I like you."

"Yeah." He burst out laughing. "And I like his kids more than I like you. So I guess we're even."

"I almost died tripping on a Lego this morning," I grumbled as we both started walking back toward the tent.

"My man, you have no idea how treacherous those damn things are. Last year, I hid them, and the twins got pissed and started putting them under my pillow whenever I stayed over. I swear those little bastards gave me nightmares. One time, I woke up and they'd put a minefield around the bed. I've prayed about a lot of weird shit. Legos disappearing should never be one of them."

I burst out laughing just as we reached the tent, and just as Abs looked in my direction. The hardness of her expression softened for an instant as her eyes zeroed in on my mouth, but the minute she saw me stare back at her, the anger returned.

So I put my hard shell back on like a freaking ninja turtle and sat down at the drum set, telling myself all the reasons I had a right to be more hurt and angry than she did.

By the time the set was done, I was exhausted.

And ready to get the hell away from Abigail and every one of those tattoos on her neck that I used to trace with my tongue.

Damn it.

Chapter Five

Abigail

The kids were adorable. It was opening day, so we ended early, and I was so thankful that I wanted to cry a bit. I needed a shower. And space.

Time away from him.

I said goodbye to everyone and got in my Jeep rental. It was white and looked like it could hold its own in the deep, white sand.

With a happy sigh, I started the engine and made my way over to The Seaside Shores condos, then hopped out.

They were adorable and perfect beach-front property. The salty wind picked up and instantly relaxed me as I took a deep breath and opened the door to the main office.

"Hi, can I help you?" The office manager looked like he was in high school. His eyes widened a bit when he saw me, and then like most people, he looked away and started rummaging.

It was a thing. What did you do with your hands? Did you wave? Point and say, "*I know who you are!*"

Meeting a celebrity was like sitting in a hot tub with a large group of people. If your hands were in your lap, you looked sketchy. If you let them float, people thought you were weird. And if you spread them wide, you were suddenly touching others and could send the wrong message.

So, this was another hot-tub moment. I broke through with my own wave and said, "Hey. I'm Von Abiga—" I shook my head at my stage name. "I'm Abigail Von Leery, and I have a reservation."

The guy visibly paled.

Crap, was I going to have another fainter?

"Are you okay?" I asked in a whisper. "Do you need water or

something?"

"Please be in there. Please be in there," he mumbled to himself as he clicked on a laptop. A bead of sweat trailed down the side of his face, and he pulled off his thick glasses and wiped his forehead then tapped away at the computer again.

I waited patiently.

He gave me a look of dread. "We don't have you down."

"Huh? What do you mean? My manager should have called."

He gulped. "I don't have your name here anywhere. Should I try your manager's?"

"Sure," I said through gritted teeth. "It's Will Sutherland." I was going to kill Will. How could he forget?

And then it hit me.

I'd changed plans last minute.

He'd sworn he'd taken care of it.

But he was going to be a new dad.

He was stressed and managing people while still performing with Adrenaline.

I knew before the guy shot me another apologetic glance that I was screwed.

I offered him a small smile. "That's okay. Do you have any rooms available?"

"It's summer." He ran his fingers through his hair. "We don't have any vacancies, especially now that we have that amazing summer camp going on for the next few months. Honestly, I don't know what to tell you other than I hope you have friends who live here or someone who can pull some strings. We were one of the only hotels to have any vacancies, but some guy this morning took our last room." He looked behind me. "Oh, there he is! Hey, Ty. So cool of you to get me tickets to—" He stopped talking.

Probably because I looked as if I were about to murder him, along with Ty.

Of course, Ty Cuban would take the last available room.

"Thought you were staying with Trevor?" I said through clenched teeth.

Ty actually looked shocked. His jaw dropped, but he recovered quickly. "Yeah, well, you try sleeping one night with three kids all under the age of seven running around screaming at all hours of the day. Let me know how that works out for you. Plus, they're like this…" He swore. "It's kind of shitty staying with the perfect family when you have none."

His confession shocked me to my core.

I couldn't breathe.

Couldn't think.

He had the band.

He'd had me.

And that was it.

His parents had died when he was young. His aunt had taken him in, but she didn't want kids—ever. Which she'd told him repeatedly until he started making enough money playing gigs at local coffee shops to help out.

And when he hit it big…

Well, that's when her love grew.

He still supported her out of love for the parents he couldn't even remember.

A flicker of respect grew as I was once again reminded how hard he'd had it. And how easy I'd had it compared to him.

I exhaled slowly and met his gaze. "I'm sorry."

"Don't be," he snapped. "I'm clearly doing just fine without your sorries." He looked back at the guy. "See ya later, Daniel."

"Bye, Ty!"

Oh, for shit's sake, the guy looked as if he'd shine Ty's shoes if he asked.

"Wait!"

I was going to regret this.

This was a bad idea.

And yet, I couldn't stop the words from tumbling out. "There was a mistake with my reservation."

Ty didn't turn around, he just froze as if I'd shocked him. "No."

"Ty, please. You won't even know I'm there. Let me just stay there for tonight. It's late, and I have nowhere to go. Your buddy Daniel says there's nothing open, and—" I started to panic as the crack of thunder filled the air.

We all had our things.

Storms were mine.

Until Ty had taught me to fall in love with my fear, rather than let it control me.

He had done that.

I felt my eyes well with tears. "Never mind. I'll sleep in my car if I have to."

"Son of a bitch," Ty snapped and turned on his heel, making a beeline for me as if I needed to either get out of the way or prepare for a fight. He jerked the duffel bag out of my hand, then reached for my other suitcase. "One night. You speak to me, I'm locking you outside on the balcony."

"Are you serious? I can't even talk?"

"Not a word."

"But what if there's a fire, and I need to yell 'fire, fire,' to save your life?"

"Let me die," he said simply. "Not a word. Swear?"

I nodded.

He tilted his head. "Already starting?"

Another nod.

"Fine. This all your shit?"

I shook my head no. Already, I could see the regret crossing his features as he held out his hand. "Keys."

I slapped them into his waiting palm and felt a bit guilty as rain pelted his body, completely drenching him as he grabbed two more larger suitcases from the Jeep and rolled them inside the building.

His white T-shirt was plastered against an insane core that literally defined every girl's fantasy when they thought of a hot rock star.

I could see some ink through the white cotton.

Was that new?

He cleared his throat.

And, like an idiot, I realized I'd been staring at his body longer than necessary. He didn't smile at me, though, or look as if he were ready to throw himself a parade because he caught me looking.

If anything, he looked even more pissed off.

I stuck out my tongue, earning an eyeball roll as he shoved past me with enough luggage to last for the next few months. I would never confess the reason for all my things, or admit the pain in my chest at watching the guy who I'd thought would be my forever touching the chaos that was my life, without even realizing I had been with a replacement the whole time.

His.

I would die before I admitted that to him.

It was hard enough admitting it to myself.

We rode the elevator in silence as water dripped off his brown hair onto the floor. When the door dinged, he remained silent as he brought my stuff down a hall with hardwood floors and bright blue paint, then stopped at the end.

He ran the keycard and kicked the door open. I was immediately hit with the smell of the ocean as a breeze picked up through the lavish condo.

It was beautiful, with bright blues, whites, and wood accents that made the furnished place look modern and welcoming. The kitchen had white granite countertops, a full gas range, and a dishwasher that I knew Zane would sell his soul before using because you know…he couldn't fix it.

It almost made me laugh, thinking about Zane.

But Zane wouldn't fix this. He couldn't.

"I'll take the guest room. You take the master." Ty stomped by me. I grabbed his arm to pull him back, but he just shoved away and kept walking. "Remember, no words. You can't argue, you can't yell. Just get your shit and try not to snore too loud."

I let out a grunt and rolled my eyes.

"Heard that." He paused at the door. "And you snore like a friggin' train unless you wear those white things on your nose, whatever the hell they're called. Remember, I know you."

His confession hung between us.

I wanted to say, "*not anymore.*"

I wanted to argue and tell him that I was different.

But the really sad part was that he was right. I was exactly the same girl that had walked away. The same scared woman who had ignored the sound of her heart breaking and made the final cut.

Because sometimes you did what you had to do to keep it from hurting worse. And I knew that loving Ty Cuban would end up destroying me.

I'd promised myself a long time ago that I would never let a man do that.

No matter how much of my heart he owned.

No matter how many parts of his I held.

Chapter Six

Ty

I could hear her breathing.

I didn't think about that. I was too focused on the words, too fixated on the anger that I kept firmly in place so I didn't do something stupid like confess everything to her. Or apologize and crawl on my hands and knees in her general direction like a total ass before I burst into tears.

Okay, so I wouldn't cry.

I wouldn't admit that the one time I did wasn't at my parents' funeral—I was too young. No, it was when Abs had walked out of my life and never came back.

Love had a way of being both the best thing that could ever happen to you and the worst thing you could feel. Because once you experienced the rightness of it, you knew exactly what you were missing when it was gone.

And there was nothing in this world that could fill that gaping hole in your soul the way love did.

Call it the science of breakups.

Nothing worked.

Not drugs.

Not alcohol.

Not music.

Not space.

Not even time. Because the memories were always there, and it was incredible how easy it was for your brain to conjure up smells, tastes, and feelings.

And since both Abigail's and my career had erupted at the same time? Everything related to music was also tethered to her.

I put a pillow over my head and yelled into it.

She was desperate. But I felt like a weak piece of shit for letting her stay with me. I hated those guys: the ones that just wanted one morsel of the girl that got away and were willing to do anything, even exchange their dicks, for a pussy. Just so they could have one last look, taste, fill, call it whatever you wanted. I hated those guys.

They sucked.

The last thing I needed was to become that guy. Because I knew if she hurt me again, I would literally have nothing left.

And it was a terrifying thought, to say the least.

I put the pillow back behind my head and turned to my side, touching the wall with my fingertips like the biggest loser on the planet. I wondered how many inches separated the space between us. If I pressed my ear to the wall, would I hear her crying because of the storm? Or was she just dreaming about stabbing me in my sleep?

It was a toss-up. I mean, it always had been with us.

The thunder cracked again, scaring the shit out of me as I jumped out of bed and shut the guest bedroom window.

This was ridiculous.

At least I wouldn't have to see her at the music camp since Drew had gone to bat for me. I was headed to Trevor's studio to help with his music students. He was so thankful that he could have more time with the kids and his new fiancée that I actually felt relief that I was finally helping and not making a mess of things.

It hadn't always been that way.

You knew there was something terrifyingly wrong when Drew, the f-up of the group, told you to put your big boy pants on.

Thunder cracked again.

Yeah, I was getting zero sleep tonight.

I grabbed my guitar on my way out to the living room, then snatched up one of my sharp number-two pencils from my satchel, along with my old, ratty, blue music notebook and sat on the couch. The front cover of the journal was almost completely torn off and had stickers from places I'd visited covering it. No matter how many times I tried to buy a new one, I still kept this one and just stapled more pages into it. Maybe it was stupid, but it was a comfort to me.

The room was dark.

Silent.

Just the way I liked it.

I loved the power behind the drums, but there was something so intimate about playing the acoustic—just me, my Gibson Les Paul, and my voice.

I strummed a few chords, switched to G, and kept strumming as my mind decided to torture me by way of memories.

So many damn memories.

"You go first." Abs laughed. "Come on, pleeeeease?"

I pointed a drumstick at her. "I can't believe I agreed to do this."

"Shut up. Yes, you can. This is what lovers do!" She sang the last part. It was one of our songs. I would kill her later. She shimmied out of her swimsuit top. Just kidding, I would maul her later and apologize for the loss of oxygen after I was done tasting.

I tossed my drumsticks onto the grass, looked over my shoulder, and then shoved down my boxer shorts and slowly looked over the cliff. "Shit, that's high."

"C'mon, all the kids are doing it, Ty!" She slapped me on the back, making me stumble toward the rocky side.

It was maybe fifteen feet high, but it was dark outside, which made it creepier. We were somewhere in Costa Rica, had no security with us, and would probably die. Hey, at least we'd be together! We'd lost security a few miles back because we needed time. Things had gotten really crazy with our band and with her new album, and I couldn't stand being in the tour bus one more hour.

This was Abs' bright idea. I would have been happy going for a walk.

She was the risk-taker. I was the one who looked like I took risks but preferred a whiskey neat by the fireplace. She was always ready to go running naked down the streets with paint on her face.

"Ready?" She was naked. So bare. Fresh ink visible down her neck. I loved the tat. I'd helped her draw it. She had done a few stars and then had them hanging from this tree as it went down her right arm. Gorgeous. So beautiful. Just like her.

"No, I'm really not." I laughed. "Why are we doing this again?"

"To prove our love?"

"Oh, so if I don't die, then it's true?"

"Exactly!" She beamed. "I knew you weren't stupid."

"Bite me." I flipped her off and then reached for her hand. "Do we count to three?"

"Aww, does the great, sexy Ty Cuban need to do a countdown to find his dick?"

"Cool. So, I'm probably drowning you when we get down there."

"If we make it."

I cursed. "Not helping, Abs."

"You go first." She nudged.

And because I was a man and needed to prove myself, I hiked up my skirt, okay not really but mentally at least, and stared down at the water. Even at night, it looked blue by the caves. "Promise you'll follow?"

"Always," she whispered. "I'll always follow you."

I jumped.

I'd thought it would scare me. Instead, a strong hit of adrenaline surged through my limbs as I flew through the air and slammed into the warm water. My first thought was: *okay, I have to do that again and make sure I do a backflip or something equally sick that we can post to social media.*

"Watch me fly!" she yelled and then jumped off, all open grins and arms spread wide. She landed a few feet from me and swam over, water cascading over her naked body. "My landing was better."

"Meh. My splash was bigger. Call it even?"

"Never!" She splashed at me playfully.

I grabbed her by the wrist and pulled her against me. "My dick's bigger than yours. There, I win."

"I have boobs." She grabbed my hands. I needed no encouragement to cup them, squeeze them with my palms, massage. Damn, I was going to drown, wasn't I? But what a great way to go.

I groaned. "You win, I surrender. Can we have sex now?"

"Aw, what a gentleman. You asked this time!" she teased, pulling away.

I jerked her back against me. I was already straining for her, pulsing with a need that I couldn't explain, and only she could satisfy. I whispered against her ear, "I love you. Even though you make me want to do this..." I shoved her down.

When she came up, she spat water in my face.

So I shoved her down again.

This went on for at least twenty minutes before we heard shouting and saw flashlight beams. We quickly swam back to the bottom of the cliff where the beach met the rocks and hid.

I'd never been colder in my life.

We held hands on that rocky beach until the flashlights were gone, and then we walked naked, hand-in-hand, to the car.

And laughed the entire way back to the tour bus.

"I just want to lay with you," I sang in a deep voice. "I just want to lay with you and hear your voice. Don't disappoint me by being a dream again. Just let me believe again..." My heart hammered in my chest as I felt eyes on me and slowly turned.

Abs was in nothing but a long, old band T-shirt—*my* T-shirt. I hated her in that moment. Hated that she would do this to me. That she would keep something that was mine, ours. Something shared.

"Who's the girl?" She walked toward me, all long legs with ink on her left thigh and a few tattoos on the top of her foot.

"I'm not sure I know her anymore," I confessed sadly as my eyes flickered to her breasts and away. Old habits. "Does it even matter?"

"I don't know."

"You're talking," I reminded her with a scowl.

She sat down across from me and propped her legs up on the coffee table. Her toenails were purple, and she had a little tiger tattoo on her big toe. "About that. It's past midnight. You said no talking, which I assumed meant until a new day. And, weird, when midnight happens, a new day begins. Crazy, I know..." She made a motion with her hands in the air. "Boom. Science."

"Boom." I flipped her off. "Leave me alone, I'm not in the mood."

"You never write at night." It almost sounded like a question. It felt a hell of a lot like prying. Easy conversation. It felt a hell of a lot like digging.

"Really?" I set down my guitar. "Do you really want to do this?"

"You'll probably lose your security deposit," she said in a challenging tone that set my body on fire. Damn it, I loved fighting with her almost as much as I loved her.

Had loved.

Past tense.

Get it through your thick skin, heart…past freaking tense.

"I'm loaded. I think I can handle a few broken dishes. You're a horrible shot, though. Do you really want the china to suffer your inability to throw like a dude?"

"All I have to do is hit one tiny, little"—she pointed her foot at my dick—"thing."

"Don't insult us both by lying about the biggest thing you've ever had in your mouth. It's not cute. It's just sad." I knew it was a low blow and that I'd basically demeaned her, but I couldn't handle it, not now. Not in the dark, and especially not during a thunderstorm.

Really, not now. Not ever.

I shot to my feet and walked past her. She reached out and grabbed my wrist. I stood there, the pain of her touch so severe, I had a hard time catching my breath. And she was barely touching me.

I wasn't ready for this battle.

For this war.

"I'm sorry," she choked out.

"Wow," I cackled. "How much did that cost you? Your soul? Oh, wait…" I jerked away from her.

"Scared," she whispered. "I got scared."

"Shit, Abs." I hung my head. "I can't just make the thunder go away. But even I'm not heartless enough to tell you 'tough shit.'" Unfortunately.

"I know."

It was too close to the memories.

Too close to home.

And yet, I couldn't be the asshole ex-boyfriend who just left her there. So I walked into my bedroom, grabbed a pillow and blanket, and then charged back out into the living room. I threw everything on the floor with all the aggression of a man who hated and hurt with the same intensity that he loved.

"T-thank you," she murmured.

"I want a ninety-minute massage for what I'm putting my body through tonight, got me? And from an actual spa. Not a little coupon you give me and sign and then never follow through on." I turned to look at her.

With a stunned expression, she nodded her head slowly. "As much as it pains me to admit this—"

"Don't," I interrupted, horrified at how fast my body heated up in all the wrong places. How could you hate someone so much but still want them the way I did?

It wasn't fair.

Life. Wasn't. Fair.

"We're adults. It's been ten years. I can handle myself." She rolled her eyes. "As long as you don't suffocate me with that pillow there..."

"Lovely daydream," I said in a sing-song voice as I jumped to my feet and stomped like an angry teen into the master bedroom. I hurled my body onto the left side of the bed and closed my eyes.

I felt the bed dip.

Heard the sound of her legs sliding along the sheets.

Tortured myself with the sighs that followed.

And only realized right before my eyes were heavy with sleep that we'd both just gone into default mode.

Me on the left, her on the right.

Me on top because I got hot, her under the sheets because she got cold.

The only thing missing were the two hearts straining toward each other.

Instead, we were two people falling asleep with broken pieces scattered around us, still searching for a way to be whole again.

Chapter Seven

Abigail

It had been years since I'd slept that well. And as luck would have it, the thunder just had to happen the night I lay in his bed.

Just like that night so many years ago.

When everything had changed.

The thunder had been so loud, the lightning like a bad omen as it slashed across the sky in warning. It had been my alert from the universe.

I turned to Ty. He was still sleeping. His hair poked up all over the place, his skin tan against the cool, white sheets. He looked so peaceful lying there, as if he didn't have a care in the world. When all I felt was the oppressive weight of what it felt like to share a bed with him.

"What?" He didn't open his eyes. "What could you possibly need this early in the morning with the monsters gone?"

I rolled my eyes, grabbed my pillow, and slammed it over his head. What could I say? He brought out the worst in me and was ruining the peace and quiet when all I wanted was to offer a ceasefire so that we could prevent murder that summer.

The pillow hit him square in the face. His eyes flashed open and then narrowed as he grabbed his own pillow and slammed it onto my body. I tried getting away, but he'd always been faster, stronger. He grabbed me by the hips and slammed me back against the mattress then straddled me, pillow held high. "It's only six a.m., and I was going to sleep in. Now, I wake up to you not only plotting my murder but also hitting me with a pillow? You really want to start this?"

I gulped. He was naked from the waist up. Glorious muscles flexed within reach of my fingertips. I didn't mean to reach out and touch his abs or to trace my finger down his chest, running along the guitar tattoo I'd helped design when we were on tour together the last time.

When everything ended.

"You didn't cover it," I whispered, my hand still pressed against his skin.

Slowly, he lowered the pillow, his face hard. "This feels like a distraction."

"Sorry." I started jerking my hand away when he snatched it in his and squeezed.

I couldn't breathe.

It was too much.

Touching him was worse than having him because it reminded me of what I was missing without him ever giving me a taste of it.

Our issues had never been our attraction to each other.

Or even the fighting.

It had been deeper than that. And yet, lying there with Ty on top of me, with him clutching my hand so tightly it almost hurt, I couldn't find any solid reason for why I'd walked away.

And that was the problem. He was good at making me forget.

Just like he was good at justifying things that were big issues.

He was all smooth words, perfect voice, playful, and protective. He was everything you wanted in a man. The only issue was that every single breathing female knew it.

And *he* knew they knew.

And he used it against them—against us.

He slowly leaned over me, his body hot as it covered mine. What was happening? And why was I letting it? He lowered his mouth to my ear and whispered, "Hit me with a pillow again, and I'm putting arsenic in your pancakes."

And just like that, I was jolted back to reality as I bucked against him and smacked him in the chest. "Why are you such a jackass?"

"Born this way." He grinned and hopped off of me, giving me an insane view of his ass in Under Armour joggers as he left the room, only to poke his head back in. "At least I have a valid reason for being what I am. What's your excuse?"

I seethed. "Excuse for what?"

"Being an all-around bitch. Abandoning people. Cutting people out of your life. Or maybe your frigid tendencies, hmm?" He shrugged. "At least I know what I am. At least I claim it. You just sit there and pretend you're without fault."

"That's not true!" I yelled, jumping to my feet as I pulled the tangled bit of sheet off the bed. "I never pretended to be anything but who I am!"

"How sad." He said it like he really meant it. "That even after a decade away, you're still the same scared girl, running in the opposite direction of everything you want just because you're too afraid to have it."

I slapped him across the face so hard, my hand stung.

He bit out a curse and stormed off.

Typical.

And yet, when I heard the shower turn on and heard him start singing like he always used to while using his pink loofah...

I felt immediate guilt, not just for slapping him.

But because I knew he was right.

And I hated that he still saw through me like that. Like he always had. As if I had nothing to lose when I had *everything* at stake.

It was easy for people like Ty, ones who just went after things blindly, willing to fight whatever monsters lay in their way. There was no logic to his decisions, only passion.

But logic kept people safe.

It made the world go 'round, right?

Ty Cuban never played it safe. And I hated that he didn't recognize why normal people had to.

The shower turned off. I made myself busy and went in search of some coffee just in time to see the man himself walk into the kitchen in nothing but a tiny, minuscule towel that looked as if it had been made for hands not bodies.

I almost ran into the fridge before stumbling a bit and grabbing a cup and turning on the Keurig.

He walked right by me, grabbed two pods, and then his own coffee cup. "Mind making me one while I get dressed?"

"You insult me and then ask for favors?" I didn't make eye contact.

"I was honest about how I feel, which I think typically gives guys points in the pro section, not the con. And since I gave you a roof over your head, I'm gonna go ahead and say, yeah, I am." He patted me on the freaking head and walked off, but not before I grabbed the edge of his towel and tugged.

It fell to the floor right between us.

"Oops." I grinned. "Sorry."

He picked it up and started twisting and wrapping it around itself.

Oh, shit.

I ran in the opposite direction just as I heard the first whip of the towel then burst out laughing when he slipped into a barstool. "Running only encourages me."

I laughed and then jumped over the couch while he sprinted after me. "Stopppp!" I felt the air whoosh next to my bare legs and then went into the bathroom and shut the door, but not before he put his foot in the opening and followed me inside.

"No place to run, Abs." His grin was menacing and beautiful. "So what will it be? Coffee? Or do you want to feel my wrath?"

He was naked.

Half-aroused.

I gulped and tried to look anywhere but at his crotch.

His grin grew.

Other things grew.

"You okay, Abs? You look a little flushed."

"It's hot," I said through clenched teeth.

"Hmm, maybe take a cold shower, I know I did. I'm only human…"

I blinked up at him. His chest heaved as he took a step closer.

Steam still filled the bathroom from his shower as I backed up against the wall. He pinned me against it, his hands on either side of my head, his lips inches from mine, the towel forgotten.

"What are you doing?" I asked in a half-whisper.

"Taking." He pressed his mouth to mine in a painful kiss, one that said exactly what was on his mind. I felt the words that were directed at me that he never got to speak out loud, all the hurt that he felt in his soul. All of that was in that kiss and the way he pressed his body against mine. He was bigger now, older, obviously. We'd been kids back then.

We were adults now.

And this was a very adult kiss.

One that made me sad because it made me think about all of the girls in the last decade who had been on the other side of it.

His tongue swirled against mine, taking, taking, taking. It seemed that was all he could do—take, not give.

So I let him.

Deep down, I knew that he deserved more than a flippant remark as I turned my back on us.

We broke apart.

Ty's blue eyes were wild.

It was terrifying.

And beautiful.

"I figured that would hurt worse." He hung his head. "Instead, I think the pain was more self-inflicted than anything…" He turned around. "I gotta go to the studio…"

I don't know how long I stayed in that spot in the bathroom, tears in my eyes.

Long enough for me to hear the door slam.

Long enough for there to be a cup of coffee waiting for me in the kitchen.

Long enough for him to leave a note that said: *Find somewhere else to stay.*

And for the first time in a long while, I sat on the couch and cried as I touched my trembling lips with my hand, remembering the way the kiss had felt.

So good.

So simple, yet so complicated.

Then again, love always was.

Because we made it that way.

Chapter Eight

Ty

"I'm an idiot," I muttered as I walked into Trevor's studio and pulled out a seat behind the recording booth.

"Tell me something I don't know," he said without looking up from the board. "But, seriously, tell me more. Did you sleep with another groupie? Walk out into the thunderstorm last night with a hairdryer? Really, I'm all ears."

I glared at the back of his gray Henley and black beanie and made a face. "Aww, is someone not getting laid?"

He spun his chair around and crossed his arms. "Me getting laid isn't the problem. Say it with me, 'commitment.'"

"Did you say that slowly for my benefit, or because you forgot how to enunciate?"

"Jackass." He rolled his eyes and grinned. "So, tell me, what did you do this time? Now I really am curious."

"Oh, you know, the usual self-sabotage...like inflicting your own wound and wondering why the hell you're bleeding all over the place. Super fun. Might do it again sometime. Spoiler alert, if she keeps staying with me, it's going to happen tonight..."

"She?" Trevor leaned forward. "Are we talking about some random girl, or the one who took your heart and lit it on fire then ran it over with her Maserati for good measure?"

"She blew up my heart with c-4, and it was a Benz. But, yeah, same girl."

"Hmm." He started tapping a pen against his jeans. "Is there a reason she's staying with you when you guys can't be in the same vicinity without resorting to physical violence and mental warfare?"

"Right, so…" I sighed and wiped my hands down my face. "It seems I have a heart. And before you laugh, remember, it's very tender. Tread lightly."

Trevor grinned. "Ah, so it came to life the minute you saw her, and you just couldn't say no?"

"More like"—I thought about it, I mean *really* thought about it—"I was exhausted. Had a moment of weakness, which she most likely recognized. She brought up a trigger, I couldn't say no. And maybe, just maybe, I like to play the hero every once in a while. The villain is so fucking taxing, you know?"

"No, not really." He burst out laughing. "Though I'm surprised you're alive without any sort of bruising or scratches. Then again, you are wearing a leather jacket, so it could be a way to cover up the marks."

"Very funny," I grumbled. "She woke me up with a pillow fight." I held up my hands. "But before you get all excited and ask if we started dancing to Tay Swift in our underwear, no, it wasn't sexy. It pissed me the hell off. I straddled her, realized that I was stuck between either murdering her with my bare hands or kissing her, freaked the hell out, and left the situation only to be faced with another low-blow. I just can't stop myself from reacting. And every time I react, my brain misfires and goes 'holy shit, man, she's flirting, kiss her, do it, do it now!'"

Trevor was quiet for a minute and then said, "I think you need therapy."

"My dick needs therapy." I crossed my arms. "I kissed her, you know."

"And did she bite your tongue off or kiss you back?"

I looked away. "Doesn't matter. I ruined it by insulting her, us, call it what you want, but I think she's driving me absolutely insane. I told her to stay somewhere else, and I'm already regretting it."

"Okay, I'll bite. Putting on the therapist hat…why do you think you're regretting it when you guys get along like oil and water?"

"Maybe because my heart recognizes she's the jelly to my peanut butter, even though she's masquerading as the worst flavor of the bunch. I mean, who really likes marmalade?"

"Nobody."

"Thank you!" I threw my hands into the air. "Nobody. I mean, could she at least *try* to be grape? Hell, I'd even take blackberry! But, no, she has to be the orange kind, and my heart doesn't fucking care because no matter how many times I recognize how wrong it is, I'd rather fight than lose her…"

Trevor's grin was huge. "You're growing up."

"You are literally two years older than me, shut the hell up."

He raised his hand. "Been divorced, have three kids, just got into my first real relationship where I feel like an adult and don't want to murder the person I'm with, finally happy… Yeah, I'd say you're where I was at a few years ago." He shrugged. "Part of this whole agreement was that you had to spend a few hours with her. My suggestion is to use this as an opportunity to see if something is still there. You might be surprised."

"Surprised?"

"Ten years is a long time, man. It's easy to project all that shit from the past into the present. But she's not the same girl anymore. You're not the same guy. You were barely at legal drinking age… Plus, what do you have to lose?"

Everything.

I was quiet.

My silence said everything because Trevor knew I didn't like it. I filled the silence with my words because I hated being alone with my thoughts. They were too deep, too scary, too…revealing.

Words were easier when you didn't have to think about them.

"I'm afraid this is it. My final concert. What happens if we don't get our encore?"

"Then you, Ty Cuban, finally grow the hell up, stop sleeping around, and move on."

"But sex is so fun," I teased.

"Nice deflection, but you know you just replaced one drug with another. Ask Alec all about that one. He was addicted to all the hard stuff, then replaced it with his girlfriend, now wife. That did not end well for him. She forgave him, and they got over it, but I wouldn't recommend trading out addictions. Demetri took up running. Maybe you need a hobby that doesn't break hearts and crush souls, hmm?"

"Maybe." I gulped. Why did my throat feel thick? Was I having an allergic reaction to the air in the studio?

Or was I actually feeling…guilty?

Shit.

Now my eyes felt watery.

I tugged at my shirt. "It's stuffy in here."

"It's okay to be emotional."

"You can stop talking anytime, Trev."

He grinned. "Fine, your first student gets here in ten minutes. Pull your shit together. You have two more after that, then some free time to start writing a few songs. I want something…sad. Think you're up for it?"

"Of course." I winked, even though I felt like my soul was screaming on the inside. Write something sad? Of course I could. Because I'd been living in a perpetual state of sadness for a decade.

I knew it well.

We were best friends.

Because Trevor was right about one thing.

I replaced things.

And just like my addictions…

I'd replaced the best friend I used to have with the only thing she left me with.

Sadness.

Chapter Nine

Abigail

"So you're going to be in charge of entertainment during lunch." Drew handed me an iPad. "These are all the requested songs from the kids. Don't botch ours, or Ty will probably murder you, especially if you sing his part like you did last time in a whiny girl voice."

I smirked. "Admit it, that was hilarious."

"Yes, so funny that he threw a chair through the window once it went viral on BuzzFeed. Couldn't find him for two days. He showed up high as a kite, and we had to cancel our concert." He glared. "But sure, hilarious."

Guilt slammed into me. "It was just a joke."

"Right, just like it was only a heart you broke."

"Don't pretend like you know everything." I seethed. "It's not fair."

Drew sighed. "Look, I've always been Switzerland. It sucks enough that we all have mutual friends and connections, but I'm starting to lean into the bro territory only because he actually likes kids, right? So the fact that he was willing to do anything so he didn't have to work next to you means he's still not over you. It means it's been a decade of hurt, and he still can't function. That's not normal."

I swallowed the hurt in my throat. "I don't even know what to say."

"Don't say...sing." He pointed me to the stage. "And do me a favor?"

"What?"

"Don't break his heart a second time. I'm not so sure he has enough pieces left for even his best friends to glue back together if you do. And, trust me, I know what it feels like to be left broken without anyone to help you. It's not a fun place to be." His gaze darkened. "And, no, I'm not telling you anything, so get that girlie look out of your eye that says '*spill*.' We aren't best friends, that title goes to Zane."

"Someone called?" Zane came up and wrapped his arm around me, then tilted his head. "Did you sleep with someone last night?"

My eyes widened.

What the hell? Did he have a sixth sense or something?

Drew's expression turned murderous and in my direction.

Perfect.

"Um, no. I just…acquired a roommate," I offered lamely.

Zane sniffed my hair and backed up. "You smell like Ty."

"I DO NOT!" I yelled, earning the attention of a few campers, who gave me terrified looks. Great, I'd just scared all the first-graders. I gave them all a weak smile and a wave, only managing to get them to turn around as quickly as they'd swiveled my way.

I was making friends fast, that was for sure.

"Sorry for yelling." I snuck a look at Drew. I hated that he looked disappointed in me, almost as much as I hated that he had struck a chord. "I'm not sleeping with him. He did let me stay in his condo for the night. It was raining, they messed up my reservation…point is, we didn't kill each other, but I got scared." Drew cursed. "And we slept in the same bed, but I was under the covers. He was on top." There, that sounded better.

Zane covered his smile with the back of his hand then said, "Did you, uh, manage to draw a line down the middle of the bed too, or did you just build a barricade with pillows?"

"Very funny." I shoved him.

"Hey!" He held up his hands. "I'm just curious. Plus, a guy like Ty doesn't really do boundaries…"

Zane didn't know.

The thunder.

The omen.

The night I'd never forget.

No boundaries was right, wasn't it?

"Hey." Drew looked suddenly concerned. "Are you okay to play?"

"Yeah." I pulled away. "Just great." I flashed them both an easy smile and walked onto the stage, pulling my guitar over my head and reaching for the mic.

"Hey, everyone. I'm Von Abigail, and I'm here to entertain you while you eat the best seafood Seaside has to offer!" Cheers erupted. "How's day two going?"

More cheers.

Kids. They were so easy.

"All right, so we're going to start with an AD2 favorite. Sing along if you know it!" I raised my hands over my head and started the tempo with my clap. The kids followed suit, all of them already jamming out as I sang the first few words.

I couldn't stop smiling as all the kids giggled and joined in.

And, for a few brief moments, I was free.

All the crap from earlier, from the past, was gone.

I was transported.

"I'm petrified." I stared at the stage I would be doing my very first headliner performance on. Ty was right behind me, holding me. I relied on him for everything.

And he took on the job like a champ. I was alone on the road, he was all I had, and since he had no family, it was like I was all his and his alone.

I loved it.

Never once felt suffocated.

I was his. He was mine. Period.

"You'll be fine," he whispered in my ear. "And if you get scared, just remember, I'll be on stage left, cheering you on after our set. All right? Plus, you've done this before."

"I've opened before. I've never co-headlined," I reminded him. At least Adrenaline was with me. At least Ty was with me.

"Do you trust me?" he asked.

"Yeah." A tear slipped down my cheek. "What if I mess up?"

"We all mess up. Yesterday, Will forgot every lyric to *Be Yours*, and it's the shortest song we have. Just rely on the fans to get you through it if you forget."

I took a deep breath. "Okay. I can do it."

Later that night, I was halfway through my set when I saw it. One of the dancers for AD2 was leaning against Ty in a way that made my inner tiger want to jump out and pounce.

I ignored it until a groupie with a backstage pass came at him with a huge hug. He, of course, hugged her back, took a picture, and kissed her on the cheek.

It was nothing.

Right?

I missed the next chord and tried to focus on my music, not on my boyfriend or the free hugs and kisses he was giving complete strangers.

The song ended.

All the kids cheered.

And I quickly went into the next one because I didn't trust myself not to look to stage left and imagine Ty right there, doing the exact same thing, stealing my focus, my heart, my soul, and making me feel like I was drowning without even being aware of it.

He was too busy making everyone happy.

Just like he was too busy taking care of me.

I swallowed the lump in my throat and flashed a smile at the crowd, then kept strumming my guitar. The music helped, it soothed. But even it didn't take away the sting of a heart that'd been bruised and broken.

In hindsight, I should have told him why.

I should have admitted the fear.

But saying it out loud to Ty meant that it had happened. It was real. And at least I had parents, right?

At least I had parents.

He didn't.

I had no right to be upset.

I still was.

And even after ending the final song for the campers, I couldn't shake the sadness and loss I felt in my soul as I walked out of the camp and down to the ocean.

"You did good," Drew said in a low voice. "Something you need to get off your chest?"

I stared at the water. "Need and want are two very different things. Do I need to? Probably. Do I want to? Absolutely not." I kicked the sand and looked down as it blew away.

"You know…" Drew starting a sentence like that was never good, not at all. "It's okay to still love him."

"Not when I'm the reason he hates me," I said in a flat voice to keep myself from bursting into tears. Because as many times as I said I hated Ty, as much anger as I felt for him, it was the only way to keep the sadness at bay. The only way to justify the actions I took.

"Maybe if you actually talk to him instead of inflicting emotional damage first, you guys can get over it."

"Ha." I gave him a funny look. "You do realize you should be looking in the mirror, right?"

He quickly looked away. "Yeah, well, one of us has been given a second chance. My second chance is already married and pregnant, so how's that for karma?"

My heart sank. "You still love her? Angelica?" She was married to Will. It was still a thorn stuck in their friendship, but they'd put it behind them for the band. I liked to think that Drew was over her, but I saw the way he looked at her every single time she and Will were together.

That sort of pain was impossible to hide, even though Drew tried. I wondered if that was the future I had, watching Ty finally settle down with a good girl, a worthy one, a woman who was braver than me, who fought for him and didn't force him to fight for her.

I hugged my legs and rested my chin on my knees.

Drew didn't answer me, he just put his arm around me as we sat there and watched the waves crash against the shore.

A few minutes later, someone joined us.

Zane.

And then Demetri.

I frowned at them both. "Shouldn't you guys be with the campers?"

"Alec's doing just fine." Demetri jerked his head in Alec's direction as he stood on the stage and strummed a few chords.

I made a face. "Music theory?"

"Those band nerds are living their best life, trust me." Demetri grinned. "Plus, we have a staff of twenty volunteers and security. He's fine."

"True." I cleared my throat.

"So…" Demetri looked over at me. "Is this an intervention, because I love the shit out of those."

Zane burst out laughing, while Drew gave me a wide smile.

"No." I shrugged. "Just talking. You know, feeling sorry for myself. It's super fun. Who wants to go next?"

"Me, me!" Zane raised his hand. "I'm out of marshmallows, I'm sad."

Demetri shoved him into the sand, while Drew cursed under his breath.

"So I've been thinking," Demetri finally said after a few seconds of fighting. "This upcoming tour could either suck the life out of all of us, or be really fun. All the wives are coming, girlfriends, fiancées." Drew's face fell. "And it would be nice if you weren't ready to kill Ty every time he speaks."

"Yeah, it would be nice," I agreed. "What are you getting at?"

"Little suggestion." Demetri shrugged. "When you're together… pretend it's new and see what happens."

"Pretend what's new?"

"Your feelings," he explained. "It's the baggage that's making everything suck between you guys. Pretend you went and exchanged it for really shiny shit that doesn't look and feel like ten years ago. You might be surprised. Oh, and I can say that because I was born with baggage, all right?"

"Maybe," I finally said.

"Good." Demetri put his hand on my knee, reaching across Zane, who gave me a serious look.

"You mean it?" Zane whispered.

"I'll try not to murder him and to…listen." I gulped.

"I'm happy for you." Zane kissed me on the top of the head.

"Yeah." Now, I just needed to figure out a way to stay in the condo without pissing Ty off again. I thought about it for a few seconds and then jumped to my feet. "Hey, does Ty still like pasta?"

"He's a guy." Drew rolled his eyes. "If it's food, he likes it."

"Except certain jam flavors." Zane shook his head. "I mean, who hates jam?"

"I hate birds so…" Demetri offered.

"You're scared of them." Drew snorted out a laugh. "Big difference. Oh, shit, run!"

Demetri screamed.

And I found that I could, in fact, laugh like I didn't hurt.

Huh, imagine that.

Chapter Ten

Ty

Demetri: *Mayday, mayday, I may…wow that's so many mays, weird.*

I looked at the text. It had been a long day of teaching, followed by writing sad songs that made me depressed as hell.

But at least I didn't have to see her, work with her, watch her laugh, wonder if her skin felt the same against mine.

Son of a bitch. Where was a mind-altering drug when you needed one? I was able to get my shit together just in time for my first guitar lesson and actually managed to enjoy my day. I forgot how much I loved teaching kids something they were as passionate about as I was. And they genuinely wanted to learn, another bonus. Plus, they looked at me like I wasn't the devil. It felt nice. Demetri still hadn't said anything. What? Did he fall asleep? I texted him back.

Me: *Please don't send warning texts and forget to actually tell me what you're warning me about.*

Demetri typed back right away.

Demetri: *I was attacked by a seagull today, so sorry if my mental focus is complete crap…I almost died.*

Alec: *The kids thought someone was getting murdered. We had to calm everyone down with ice cream. Demetri included.*

Demetri: *Thanks, man.*

Ah, the notorious group texts. I loved them when I wasn't the subject. I waited for someone else to pipe up.

Will: *Even though I'm not there, I really appreciate the accurate video footage I was sent by Drew. I mean, if that isn't friendship, I don't know what is.*

Drew: *Baby steps…*

And cue awkward silence.

Me: *Is there a reason for all of this?*

Zane: *I'm up, so I talked with your girl. Well, we all did. Demetri called it an intervention of sorts. But really, it was more of a stop being stupid and act your age talk, kind of like the ones we have with you on an hourly basis.*

I sent them all a middle finger emoji.

And got several back.

I sighed and pulled my jacket tighter around my body as I made my way to the condo, trying to walk and text at the same time.

Trevor: *I think I made Ty cry today.*

Me: *Son of a bitch, that conversation was in the vault!*

Demetri: *Conversation? What conversation?*

Lincoln Greene has entered the conversation.

Jamie Jaymeson has been added by Demetri Daniels.

Worst. Day. Ever.

Lincoln was an actor, best friends with all of us, but he was back in LA shooting a film with none other than our other friend, actor and director, Jamie Jaymeson.

And now that everyone's caught up…

Lincoln: *Saw the video. I thought Demetri was going to shit himself. Also, I'm guessing I was added because we have more juicy Ty/Abby updates?*

Jaymeson: *Juicy. I really appreciate the play-by-plays, Zane. Truly.*

Me: *I'm so glad you're all entertained by my life. Don't you have wives? Kids? JOBS?*

Demetri: *Trevor made Ty cry, and now you're all caught up. Ready? Discuss!*

I was almost to the condo. A chill wracked my body as I imagined sitting in my room alone tonight. I was alone a lot, why was tonight any different?

Because Abigail had reminded me what it was like to be part of something special. Something real. *Damn it, Abs. Why now?*

Alec: *He's still in love with her.*

Trevor: *Nooooo, really?*

Drew: *For what it's worth, she was sad today too…thus the intervention. She may, uh…try to mend the broken fences.*

Zane: *All the fences.*

Demetri: *Let's hope she uses something other than superglue, though from our convo, I think it's going to be a good night for you.*

Lincoln: *I saw her last year at the Emmys, she looked good.*

Jamie: *She helped on the soundtrack to my last movie and gave free puppies to a few of the kids on set.*

Me: *If this is your way of trying to convince me she doesn't hate the world, it's not working. I already know she likes everyone but me, thus the reason I wasn't enough for her to stay.*

And...silence. Way to make it awkward, Ty!

I groaned into my hands and looked down at my phone.

Someone was typing.

Drew: *Just...try.*

Alec: *Do it for us.*

Demetri: *Do it for the fans.*

Jamie: *Do it for the puppies.*

I smiled at that.

Me: *I hate all of you.*

Zane: *Bullshit, you love us.*

Me: *I'm almost back to the condo, the lights are on, I think I'm either being robbed, or you should have been more clear with your warnings. Is she still there?*

Trevor: *Quick, Demetri, a bird, duck!*

Demetri: *Gotta go!*

I glared. And...silence.

No more texts.

Nothing.

Me: *Bastards.*

I slid my phone back into my pocket and jerked open the lobby door, making my way down the hall towards the elevator.

I knew before I even got into the condo.

She was there.

I could feel it in my skin, burned onto my heart.

She hadn't left.

I couldn't decide if I was happy, nervous, sad, confused, or all of the above.

I ran my key card over the door and pushed it open.

And there she was.

My nightmare.

My love.

Von Abigail, or to me, just Abs, jeans-clad ass high in the air as she pulled something out of the oven. Her hair was piled on top of her head, all wild and carefree, her makeup was light, her lipstick dark red. She wore a crop top that said *Tokyo* that had little cutouts to reveal more skin than my eyes were prepared for.

"Please tell me you wore something more appropriate for the kids," I grumbled as I made my way into the condo and dropped my bag on the couch.

My stomach growled as I greedily looked at the spread of garlic bread, spaghetti, and some sort of salad with nuts on it. Next to that, a glass of wine.

Wine?

I narrowed my eyes. "Giving alcohol to an addict."

"Alcohol was never your problem. Filling that void in your soul was," she said under her breath and then looked up and flashed me an apologetic smile. "Sorry, it just came out."

"Happens," I said gruffly. "And also accurate." I pulled out a barstool. "Are we having company?" I reached for the garlic bread, only to get my hand slapped. "Ouch!"

"It's not ready yet." She pointed a knife at me. Ah, memories. "And, no, I did this for you as a thank you for letting me stay last night." She cleared her throat. "And for maybelettingmestaytonighttoo…"

"Yeah, you're going to have to talk slower. Repeat that last part."

"For letting me stay tonight, too." She was so damn quiet, I still didn't catch it. I was worried it was what I thought it was. Was this why the guys had warned me?

"Abs." I groaned. "Look at me and say it again so a normal human can hear."

"You're not a normal human, ergo, I have to try all possibilities." She opened her mouth.

I clapped a hand over it before she could get any words out. "If you start speaking in another language, I'm eating the bread and then putting spaghetti in your bra." I leaned over and took a peek. "No bra. Right, too constricting. Okay, I'm putting it in your thong."

Her eyes heated.

My hand felt that heat.

"Shit." I pulled my hand away. "Must you torture me? You aren't wearing underwear, are you?"

She gulped. "My jeans are too tight. And before you make some offhand comment about my ass or eating habits, remember, I'm holding a knife."

I held up my hands in surrender. "I like your ass. Hey, do me a solid. I forgot what it looks like, give us a turn?"

She scowled.

I burst out laughing. "All right, so what were you saying before I got distracted by boobs and ass?"

She actually blushed.

How I was able to have a normal conversation without launching my body across the breakfast bar was a miracle that deserved an Olympic medal or least a nod toward sainthood.

Abs took a deep breath. "I would like to discuss the possibility of me staying with you for the next few weeks."

My jaw dropped. "Did you just...ask instead of tell?" Why wasn't she yelling? Why wasn't I threatening? Stunned, I just stared at her.

She gulped and looked down at her hands as she wrung them. "I figure I can cook our meals to make up for it and also pay for half, even though I know you're loaded, blah blah blah. It would make me feel better."

I still couldn't speak. I just stared at her with suspicion in my soul. Then again, she'd put the knife down, so this really wasn't a threat, was it?

I pointed at the food. "And this...this happens every night?"

"Every night." She grinned.

"Real food?" I felt my eyes start to water. Damn those allergies to hell. Seaside really needed to do something about the air vent systems. But, come on, real food!

"And..." She rounded the corner. I watched the sway of her hips like a man starved, because, duh, I felt starved almost every day of my life. I hated eating out with a passion. "I'll even take suggestions."

I reached out to her before realizing what I was doing, put my hands on her hips and pulled her in between my legs. "What's the catch?"

"No catch." She put her hands against my chest, her palms flat. My throat went completely dry. "Just let me have a bedroom, and I promise I'll offer earplugs if I really do start to snore."

"Start?"

She rolled her eyes. "Fine, when I snore."

"Better." I didn't want to let go.

We were at another standstill.

"So?" She licked her cherry-red lips. "Is that a yes?"

"Depends. Did you or did you not drug my food?"

She laughed. "Guess you'll have to try it to find out."

"I can see *Dateline* now. Ex-girlfriend kills member of Adrenaline: death by garlic bread."

"Meh, I'd probably put it in the sauce."

I eyed the sauce with suspicion. "That's not helping."

She rolled her eyes, reached over my body to dip her finger into the sauce and licked it right off. "See?"

"You could have a tolerance," I pointed out.

She took another swipe, then dipped her finger in again. This time, I caught it and brought it to my lips and licked it off.

I couldn't decide what tasted better, her skin or the sauce.

Her eyes dilated.

I dropped her hand. "Fine, on one condition."

"What?" She looked ready to hug me. I felt my body lean toward hers in anticipation.

"This counts as our ceasefire. You tell the guys that you staying with me means I don't have to report back with what we did for our three hours a day, all right? We are officially all even." I held out my hand.

"Three hours a day?" She tilted her head.

I sighed. "That was my deal from the guys, I had to try." I made air quotes. "But this is better because I get food, also my hand's dangling between us like a rejected modifier, yes or no?"

She nodded her head, then took my hand.

And then I pulled her into my arms and gave her a hug. "Thank you for asking."

She sagged against me, defenses gone. I wondered what it would be like to finally have that girl back, the one who didn't attack first and ask questions later. She'd always had a temper, but as years went on, it had turned into this I-hurt-you-first-so-you-don't-hurt-me thing. It was the cause of so many arguments, and she never told me why. I always blamed myself.

Even when she'd said she was just going through some things.

Her parents had divorced, but they were still really supportive of her, so I could never for the life of me understand why a girl who had it all acted like someone had broken her in half.

"Welcome," she whispered against my neck.

I tensed at the feeling of her breath on my skin.

Too late, she pulled back and made her way around the breakfast bar, grabbing a plate and piling it high with food. My stomach did a stellar job of distracting both my brain and my heart from the conversation. I dug in with fervor and almost proposed.

Then felt my stomach clench.

Ha, been there, done that. And wonder of all wonders, she slept in the T-shirt.

I let out a growl of frustration.

"Is the food okay?" She looked worried.

"It's perfect, Abs," I said honestly. "I just ate too fast."

"Some things never change," she teased, not realizing it just made me feel even sicker.

"Yeah." I offered a small smile. "Why don't I clean up a bit and you can tell me all about the bird video."

She burst out laughing. "Demetri was attacked."

"That guy really needs to get over his fears. They're more afraid of him than he is of them."

"Right, but Zane had put a piece of bread in Demetri's hoodie, thus the aggressiveness of the bird."

I burst out laughing. "Oh, tell me he screamed like a girl. Nobody sent it to me yet."

"What's your number?" She laughed. "I'll text it."

My throat closed up again.

Why would I change my number?

Funny story...I couldn't bring myself to do it.

Because I was waiting for the day that her name would flash across the screen. Had dreamt about the moment and then hated her more each day that it didn't happen.

"It's the same," I said in a gravelly voice.

Her eyes shot to mine. So many questions. "Oh, okay."

Well, that was my answer, wasn't it? She hadn't even tried calling on someone else's phone just to hear my voice or to check in on me.

Ten years of hope.

Wasted.

The room went from relaxed to tense as she quickly sent me the video. I felt my cell buzz in my pocket and was transported back to all the times I prayed it was her and was disappointed when it wasn't.

So many countless women.

So many drugs. So many things that did nothing but make the ache grow.

I pulled out my phone and set it on the counter, then went about cleaning everything up, storing the food in plastic containers.

We worked together in silence.

And then I gave her a quick hug to say thank you. "I need to write, so I'll just be in my room, okay?"

My fight had officially left me.

I'd spent so many years keeping the anger in front of me like this giant shield that I forgot all about hope and how it was the strongest shield of all. It was the reason I could even feel the anger.

But now that the hope felt shattered?

The anger wasn't strong enough to take its place.

It was too bruised, wasn't it?

Because anger was just another name for fear, rejection, and sadness all wrapped up in one shiny package.

My fight had left.

The last thing that had separated her from me. And now? All I had was the music to keep me sane. Either that, or default and find some local girl to bang.

But even that didn't sound like it would do anything except make me more depressed. So I walked numbly back to the guest room, grabbed my guitar, and started to play.

Chapter Eleven

Abigail

I messed up.

I wasn't sure how or when it actually happened over the course of the meal, but we went from joking and actual conversation to him completely shutting down. And as much as I wanted to blame his typical Ty Cuban temper, he wasn't angry.

He looked devastated.

Hurt.

My throat burned as I stared at his closed door.

I'd made dessert but was afraid to rock the boat even more. Why couldn't I do anything right when it came to him? I was trying, shoving out that olive branch and attempting not to wave it in front of the pissed-off bull.

Gathering up some courage, I went over to the fridge and pulled out the tiramisu. I knew it was his favorite, even though it was store-bought. He hadn't touched his wine for obvious reasons. I knew his triggers, each and every one of them. Wine had never done the trick. If anything, it just made him fall asleep after a few sips.

I grabbed my glass in one hand and a plate in the other and slowly walked over to the white door.

It's just a door.

Just one door.

And your first love, sitting on the other side, feeling things because you messed

everything up like you always do.
No big deal.

Arghhh.

I kicked the wood with my foot then winced. It sounded louder than I predicted, more aggressive. Like I was angry again.

It slowly opened to reveal a shirtless Ty with his arms crossed, his sweats slung low on his hips, Calvin Klein underwear making their appearance near the very deep V of his abs.

He was gorgeous.

Would it have been so hard for him to just…you know, let himself go?

"Hey." My voice cracked.

"What's up, Abs?" His eyes flickered from mine to the plate then back up. "You're still hungry?"

I narrowed my eyes. "No, not really. I just bought your favorite cake and figured you might want some. I mean, it's not homemade…"

He chewed on his lower lip, his face pensive as he took the plate from my hands and mumbled a thank you before moving to close the door again.

"Wait!" I spoke too soon. What was I going to say? "*Sorry for upsetting you. Again.*"

He stared me down. And for the first time, I didn't recognize the look he gave me. I couldn't read him. I'd never seen that look before. It wasn't his typical hatred or even his narcissistic smirk.

It was just…blank.

The whole face.

I suddenly felt like someone had punched me in the stomach and then kicked me off the balcony for good measure. It was like he was finally letting me see the hurt behind the mask, and it evoked the worst feeling I'd ever felt in my entire life.

Worse than walking away and crying myself to sleep.

Worse than all those times I'd seen his face flash across the media with a new model on his arm.

It was a million times worse.

I opened my mouth, but all that came out was, "I hope you like it."

If possible, his face fell even more. "I'm sure I'll love it."

The door closed.

I stood there and stared at the white wood, wondering how many fights had taken place in that room, by that door. How many kisses, how many laughs, how many tears? None of that emotion compared to how he was feeling, how *I* was feeling, seeing that.

Seeing the real Ty Cuban staring back at me like that.

And instead of all my old insecurities flooding back, I felt shame. So much shame that it was hard to catch my breath. And when it was hard to breathe, I needed to sing, touch my guitar, write, do something.

I went to my room, grabbed my guitar, then went back on the couch and started strumming out a few notes.

It didn't take long for it to start like it always did when I played the song. The same one I'd written the night of our breakup. The night I'd thrown everything away.

The night I'd made the choice for both of us because I knew it was best for his career, for mine. For his heart, for mine.

Selfish. So selfish.

I set down my guitar and grabbed my phone as a few stray tears ran down my face. My mom answered on the second ring.

"Abigail? Is everything okay?"

I sniffed. "Yeah, yeah, you know me, just singing. I get emotional."

"Oh, honey, you're just like me."

Didn't I know it?

"Yeah." My throat constricted. "How are things?"

Her sigh was long, it said more than words. "Oh, you know, your dad's on bimbo number five. She's your age. I'll at least admit she has a nice rack." She laughed. "I wish he didn't have such a wandering eye, but we can't change the flirts in our life, can we?"

I stared at the door. "I don't know…"

"What's really wrong, Abby?"

"Do you remember Ty Cuban?"

She cursed. "The guy who broke your heart?"

I shrugged, even though she couldn't see me. "He didn't necessarily do anything wrong, Mom…" It was like a repeat of our last conversation.

"The man was a walking, talking manwhore, just like your father. You found him kissing a backstage dancer, groupies, I mean…the list you gave was long and extensive."

"He always pushed them away," I said defensively.

"Oh, honey, you made the right choice. I don't want you to end up like me, with a broken heart because you didn't trust your gut. He never loved you…not if he let other women touch him."

My mind was fuzzy as it conjured up all the times he'd pushed the girls away or got an annoyed look on his face before flashing a perfect smile. "Maybe he was just a really good actor?"

"You don't need to defend him, Abby…"

"Right. But, Mom, what if I was wrong about him? What if he wasn't cheating? What if our future was solid? What if I didn't see what I thought I saw?"

"Honey, you were already growing apart. The band was just breaking out. Do you really think it was going to get better? Do you really think that he wouldn't eventually start using like the other members of the group? Or cheating?"

She had a point. Because he *did* start using.

But I blamed myself for that, too.

"Ty wasn't like Dad, Mom…" He wasn't like my father, whom I loved, but who never seemed to fill that void in his life once he left my mother for someone younger. Had I gotten them confused? My dad was a good guy. Ty had been a good guy. But he hadn't seen, he didn't know. "Walking in on them was the worst thing I've ever seen…" I said in a choked voice. No girl should have to walk in on her dad with someone younger. No daughter should have to recognize the face as the girl who hit on her boyfriend the day after—the same girl who'd kissed him.

It hit too close to home.

"Oh, sweetheart." Mom sniffled. "I know, I tried so hard, but you know men…they take and they abuse the power and love they have." Yeah, but did they? Would Ty?

"Yeah." I sighed. "All right. Well, I'm going to go to bed, okay?"

"Happy dreams, sweetie!"

"Night, Mom."

I set my cell on the table and then felt like I was being watched. I slowly turned to the left to see Ty standing, plate in hand, with such an intense look of anger on his face that it almost made me sprint in the opposite direction.

"What. The. Ever. Loving. Fuck?" he seethed. "Did I just overhear?"

Well, at least he was angry again.

So very, very angry.

"How much did you hear?" I asked in a small voice.

"Oh, you know, only enough to want to murder both your parents, bury their bodies, then shake you until you understand that I would never, *ever* cheat on someone that I loved, especially with groupie skanks who just want a piece of me so they can post it on Instagram. I mean, what the hell, Abs? I knew your parents had divorced, but this? This is why I've spent a decade in misery? *This* is why I spent countless hours hating you? Because you were scared?"

When he put it that way, I felt even worse. The sickness in my stomach roiled until I felt like I couldn't breathe. "We were so young."

"Bullshit. Love doesn't recognize ages. Try again." His gaze landed on me.

"I caught my dad with a girl my age, the same one I saw at our concert the next day kissing you. And yes, you always pushed them away, but you liked the attention. You basked in it. You never wanted to upset your fans, so you played into it, and it was only a matter of time before you broke my heart!"

"So you broke mine first?" he roared. "Are you kidding me right now?"

"No, I mean...yes. But that's not everything!" I stood and slammed my hands against his chest. "I saw!"

"Saw? Saw what? Me getting hit on? Again? It happens on a daily basis when you're a rock star!"

"NO!" I screamed. "I saw you getting high with Drew!"

His face fell as he shook his head. "So I make one mistake at twenty-two and, boom, we're done? We don't even talk about it?"

"You don't remember," I whispered. "Do you?'

"Remember what? Getting high?"

"The thunder." I started to shake. "Why I'm afraid of thunder."

He rolled his eyes. "Of course I do. It was the end of our summer concert series, the final leg of the tour. There was a huge thunderstorm, you were bawling in your hotel room, and I came and slept with you. You said it was loud and you were scared of all the fans that had tried to attack you earlier in the day. Things were getting really crazy for all of us, it was totally understandable."

"No." I felt my body sway. "I mean, yeah, that time... But I'm talking about the other time when I went to tell you I was late, and you laughed about hoping it was yours."

His face paled. "What?"

"You laughed!" Tears blurred my eyes. "And you said, 'hope it's mine,' in front of Drew and a bunch of dancers I didn't know. And then you passed out, high as a kite, and didn't remember it the next day. I ran out into the thunderstorm and got disoriented. Thankfully, our manager was out talking on his cell phone and waved me over. I took a test, it was negative, and the next day, you didn't say anything about it. Just pretended like it didn't happen."

He looked ready to puke. "Because I didn't remember it happening."

"Right." My teeth clenched. "Because you were spiraling already, and I knew it was only a matter of time before you ended up just like my dad!"

"Bullshit! I'll own up to being a complete dick, but you don't just run away from someone you love because they do something shitty. You work it out. You hold them accountable. You don't run!"

"What else was I supposed to do? Stick around and cross my fingers?" I roared.

He reared back as if I had just slapped him. "What were you supposed to do?" He hung his head and turned towards his door then looked over his shoulder. It was a look I would never forget. "You were supposed to believe in me...the way no one else did—the way no one else ever will in my life. That's what you were supposed to do."

"Ty—"

"The day you left..." His voice cracked. "I had a ring in my pocket. You didn't see it, of course...it was sweaty, between my two fingers. I was ready to get down on one knee and beg you to marry me. I was ready to leave the fame behind because I knew it was ruining me. I was ready for a family. Ready for you. And...now." He shut the door behind him so quietly that it felt like a slam.

I ran into my room and sobbed.

Chapter Twelve

Ty

"What crawled up your ass and died?" It was the first thing Trevor said to me when I walked into the studio and threw my guitar case on the floor along with my bag. I'd slept like shit, looked like shit, felt like shit.

Spoiler alert: everything was fucking shit.

"Forget marmalade flavor. She went from barely tolerable to a glass of vegemite all within the span of a single conversation with her mom. And the worst part?" I threw my hands up into the air. "I used to love her mom! I mean, what the hell? I sent her a Mother's Day card, with roses, mind you, and even asked her dad permission to marry her! And this? *This* is how they repay me? By punching me in the dick?"

Trevor made a face.

"Whatever." I ignored him. "You don't have any hard drugs in here, do you? Rubbing alcohol? Mouthwash?"

Trevor still stared.

I kept talking.

"I don't want to talk about it anymore."

"Okay." Trevor nodded slowly as I sat down, only to shoot back up onto my feet and stomp over to my guitar and jerk it out of its case.

"I don't get it. I mean, we all make mistakes. I wasn't perfect. I'm still not perfect, but you don't just abandon someone you love because you're scared. You fight for them. You fucking dig your feet in, your nails, your teeth if you have to. You don't just give up." Rage filled my line of vision as I grabbed my guitar and slammed it against the chair, causing a fine dent in the front of it and sending the chair spiraling backwards.

"Feel better?" Trevor asked in a bored voice a few minutes after the incident.

"No." I grunted and then slammed the guitar down again.

"How about now?"

"I hate her."

"You don't hate her."

"Tell my,"—I slammed the guitar onto the ground—"that!"

I didn't realize I had an audience until I heard a throat clear. Slowly, I turned to see Drew giving me a concerned look as he ushered a kid of maybe ten into the studio. "Everything okay?"

"Of course," Trevor said smoothly. "Ty was just testing the durability of his two hundred-thousand-dollar guitar." He eyed the pieces on the floor and the solid part in my hand. "Good to know you can go full rock star on a Gibson and it will still semi hold up. Right, Ty?"

"Right." I sucked in a breath and tossed the neck of the guitar to the floor. "It's important to make sure your instruments are always..." I gulped as the boy gave me a wide-eyed look. "Solid. Right, Drew?"

"Yeah, I go full rock star at least once a month." He smirked and then mouthed, "*You okay?*"

I shook my head no. "Anyways, I'll just borrow one of Trevor's acoustics, and we can get started. What's your name?"

"Connor," the kid said in a proud voice. He had shaggy brown hair, was wearing one of our band T-shirts, and had shoes with holes in them. I immediately wanted to buy him a brand-new set of kicks but figured that would be weird since he barely knew me and probably thought I was a serial killer now that I'd destroyed a guitar in front of him.

"Cool name, bro." I offered a wide smile. "Let's head into the studio, yeah?"

He shrugged.

Ah, ten-year-olds.

Was I ever that young?

Memories slammed into me, recollections of playing at every single venue I could find just so I could escape my home life. Not that it was anything exciting. My aunt didn't care until I started raking it in.

I played my first coffee shop at this kid's age and could have easily gotten kidnapped if someone would have given me a home-cooked meal. Yup. Would have walked right into that van and said, "*thank you.*"

"Is your guitar gonna be okay?" Connor asked once I gave him a stool to sit on and grabbed a chair of my own.

I smiled. "Yeah, man, like the guys said, we do that all the time to make sure that the durability of the wood will last through the entire tour." Talking out of my assssssss.

"Cool, should I do it, too?" He started lifting his guitar over his head.

"No!" I put my hands out and pulled the instrument back down to his lap. "Let's maybe just focus on some chords before you go full rock star. It's kind of like going full hulk. Once you do it, it's almost impossible to go back."

"Ohhhhhh." He nodded his head. "Cool."

"I like you, kid, you get my Marvel references," I teased.

"Marvel is better than DC."

"Except for Wonder Woman," I pointed out.

He laughed. "She's pretty."

"You blushing, bro?"

"No." He looked away. His cheeks were pink, and I couldn't hold in my laugh as he kicked my chair.

"All right, all right." I smiled. "Let's start with something simple. I always teach people *With or Without You* by U2 because it's one of the easiest songs to play on the guitar. You like U2?"

"Yeah!" He seemed excited.

"Let's do it." I forced myself to forget about the fact that I'd just ruined one of my favorite guitars in a fit of rage, in front of a child no less. I forced myself to think about the music and nothing but.

And, Abigail?

Well, she could just burn in hell for all I cared.

I was hurting.

A part of me was at least able to acknowledge that, but the anger was back, and I was actually relieved that it was because it was a hell of a lot better than that hopelessness I felt last night when I realized that I'd pined for someone for over a decade—someone who never even gave me a second thought.

The girl that got away.

Actually did.

Damn, that ached.

Burned.

Made it hard to breathe.

Because I knew that a part of me had always held on to hope that things would work out. That the story would have this magical ending of our own making. That the universe would do me a solid because I'd turned my life around. But, no, the universe didn't care about me. Who was I? Compared to everything else going on?

Maybe God was too busy for me.

"Like this?" Connor asked.

"Yup, just like that." I positioned his hands and showed him how to strum, giving him one of my pics.

The time flew by.

An hour later, I was helping him pack up and waiting for my next kid when Trevor walked in and announced that I'd had two cancelations because of summer colds.

Which basically meant that I had zero distractions until dinnertime with the rest of the crew.

Perfect.

I wanted to rage again, but I had nothing to hit that didn't cost six figures. Plus, I was half-owner in the record company, and I knew how much the equipment cost.

Connor moved past both of us to the door and poked his head out. His face said it all, no words were needed. It freaking felt like Santa had passed him over for Christmas.

"Everything okay, man?" I walked up to him and gave him a slight nudge with my body.

"No. Yes. I mean, yeah." His forced smile made my chest ache. Forget my shit, this kid was hurting. I leaned down and looked him in the eyes. They were either watering, and he was suffering from the same A/C effects as I was, or he was about ready to cry.

"It's okay to talk about things," I said softly.

I barely got that sentence out before he launched his body into mine and wrapped his arms around my waist, bursting into tears.

Trevor looked ready to break off a part of his heart and hand it over when I gave him a slow shake of the head, letting him know I would take care of it.

I hugged Connor back and waited for him to stop shaking, and then I asked the question I wished someone had asked me when I was young and hurting. Hell, I would have loved that question last night. "Bud, are you okay?"

"No." He sniffled and pulled back.

"How can I help?" I went down on my haunches so he was standing above me. I wanted to give him more power, not less, and something about getting on someone's level did that to a person—especially a small kid.

"You can't." His shoulders crumpled forward. "My dad…today was his day. He didn't come last time. And last month, he was with his new family," he spat. "And he promised. We were supposed to go to the aquarium. I mean, I've been a million times, but it was"—his lower lip wobbled—"it was with him."

I felt like an elephant was sitting on my chest. "Well, I know I'm probably not as cool as your dad, but if it's okay with your mom, I can take you."

His face lit up like a Christmas tree. "Really? But you're famous! And you were testing guitars, remember?"

Ah, one hundred and seventy-five thousand dollars down the drain. How could I forget? "Right, well, I can guitar test another day. Today, we should chill or something. You like taffy?"

He made a face. "Taffy's for kids."

"Oh, right." I held my laugh in. "We could go get a couple root beers, maybe check out some girls on the boardwalk."

He burst out laughing and then sobered. "I already have a girlfriend, I mean kinda."

"Lucky." I used my best Napolean Dynamite voice and earned another laugh.

"You know, I could probably help you get one," he said, dead serious. Man had a point.

"I'm just having some me-time for now, bro."

"That's what guys who don't have girlfriends say."

Was that pity on his face?

The tables were suddenly turned. "Right, well, let's text your mom and get her permission, then you can show me how to up my game. How's that sound?"

"Perfect!"

We texted his mom, got the go-ahead along with a tearful thank you, and set out on our day of fun. Thankfully she worked at the local school and already knew Trevor really well so she wasn't panicky over a stranger taking her son out, especially since Trevor vouched for me via text as well.

I was suddenly grateful that my other students had colds because Connor not only had better game than I did, but he was also freaking hilarious.

I told him I was going to be his new best friend.

And he laughed in my face.

Humbling, to say the least.

A few hours into our excursion, I realized I probably needed to meet everyone for dinner within the next few minutes or I'd be late.

"Well." I checked my phone. "It looks like our day of fun is almost over." I gave him a wink. "I have a dinner thing with the rest of the guys."

His face fell.

Shit.

"You could come if you want." I threw it out there and made a mental note to text his mom and let her know he'd be late.

"Really?" He perked up.

"Absolutely. Hope you like French fries." I gave him a shove, then led the way down to the Seaside Brewery. Not only did they have the best fish and chips, but their fries were enough to sell the kid for. I mean, not really, but…sort of.

We showed up about five minutes late, which was fine since I was notoriously late to everything. Trevor waved me over. He had his kids with him, along with his new fiancée, Penelope. In fact, it seemed everyone had their families with them—kids, wives, the whole works. I sighed as old feelings hit me square in the chest. There had once been a time when that was all I wanted. All I cared about. All I looked forward to. It sucked when the only person you had left didn't even call you on your birthday, and days later, asked for a new car. I shoved the feelings away and pasted a smile on my face as Trevor's kids smiled up at me.

"Ah, Lego killers, hello." I waved at the twins and his beautiful little girl who always seemed to have something stuck in her hair regardless of how hard Trevor tried to keep it from happening. It was hilarious. I lived for his stories because it was him and not me but also because I legit liked it when people were good parents.

It made it seem like maybe I'd taken one for the team during my childhood so that others could have love. You know?

Drew was sitting across from Zane. Alec and Demetri were hovering over a basket of fries. And then there was Abs, seated on the far end. Since we'd already decided the universe didn't care, it only made sense that the last two chairs left were right across from her.

"Let's go, man." I ushered Connor by the guys, making introductions as we went and then helped him plop into a seat.

I was about to open my mouth when he blushed and said, "Hey, there," to Abs in a way I swear I would never be able to perfect or accomplish. The hell?

"Bro." I elbowed him. "You have a girlfriend. What's all this talk about loving her forever because she gave you a Ding Dong?"

Connor just shrugged. "People grow out of love, Ty." Honest to God, his hand came down on my shoulder as if he were giving me the sex talk. "It's okay."

I pressed my lips together to keep from bursting out laughing and gave him a very serious nod. "Got it."

"So." Connor turned back to Abs, who looked ready to scoot her chair closer. Her face softened, and I forgot all about my anger because it wasn't about me anymore or even her, it was about this sad kid whose dad was a dick and deserved to get shot. "I like your last album."

Abs' smile was so bright, it hurt to look at her. She twisted the straw in her soda and leaned in. "Tell me more about how awesome I am."

"Girl, I could talk all day." He winked.

We now had the attention of everyone at the table.

"He has more game than you." This from Zane.

I flipped him off behind Drew's back and got another middle finger in return.

"I like this one," Abs declared. "I think we should give him backstage tickets for our concert this winter, all in favor?"

"Objection!" Drew laughed. "He says he likes you, what about us?"

"You aren't pretty." Yup, he said that in a deadpan voice that had the entire table rolling. Because let's be honest, Drew was a lot of things, and pretty was at the very top of the list.

He gaped. "Bro, I'm wounded!"

"You're fine." Connor shrugged and then looked up at me. "Hey, since we're best friends now, do you think I can get a Coke?"

My throat got tight. "Yeah, man, order whatever you want, all right? And then I think we should take a picture with everyone and send it to your old man so he knows exactly the sort of awesomeness he's missing out on."

Connor stood and threw his arms around me. "Thanks for being my friend today."

"Not just today, man." I hugged him back. "Whenever you need me."

I locked eyes with Abs and didn't miss the tear she wiped away from her cheek or the look of complete sadness that followed.

I wasn't sure if it was Connor or me.

Maybe it was just everything.

But it was the first time someone had declared me their best friend in a decade and meant it.

I held it close.

Because, sadly, as a rock star, sometimes moments like that were all you had. You had no choice but to collect them and hold them tight. Keep them forever.

Chapter Thirteen

Abigail

It had been the worst day of teaching I'd had since arriving in Seaside a few days ago. And I only had myself to blame and the fact that I'd hurt Ty without even realizing it.

My mind was jolted.

Stunned, actually.

He had been about to propose.

To me.

He had planned to leave it all behind. For us.

I couldn't fathom it.

Was afraid to even travel down that road because I knew it would be painful. Had I been that wrong about him? That wrong about us? I'd made so many stupid assumptions.

And now I was sitting in the condo, wondering how the hell I was going to approach this, apologize, and discuss it all without bursting into tears.

The hurt was equal.

But I was the one who had started it, not Ty. No, he had wanted to finish it, start a new life.

And seeing him with Connor yesterday had only solidified how incredible of a dad he would be.

I could have had that.

We could have had that.

Regrets sucked. They made you replay every conversation, every choice, and then taunted you with the what-could-have-beens.

I was sick of it.

The shower turned off.

I knew Ty would prance around with a towel wrapped around his waist. He'd probably go to the fridge and grab some juice, give me an I-hate-you look, then go back to his bedroom and slam the door.

It had been that way since we got home last night from dinner. And today was no different.

He was still mad.

And he no longer had a kid to soften the blow.

It was going to get ugly.

Because neither of us knew how to control our tempers beyond just yelling and hoping that the other didn't yell louder.

The door to the bathroom opened, and Ty—as predicted—walked into the kitchen and poked his head into the fridge, pulled out a carton of orange juice, took a few swigs, then slammed the fridge shut and started making his way by me.

He had the tiny towel on again.

I wanted to burn that towel.

Anger hit me fast and swiftly.

We needed to talk, but all I felt was this pulsing awareness of him. That and the anger that he wouldn't speak to me in private but was totally fine speaking to me in public.

I wished he would stop pretending almost as much as I wished he would just yell at me again. Tell me how awful I was. At least then, it would be a reaction. Something.

He was just passing me on the couch when I did it.

I couldn't explain why I thought it was a good idea, I just reacted, jumped to my feet and onto his back, wrapping my arms and legs around his slick torso.

"What the ever-loving hell are you doing?" he roared, trying to shake me off.

Be the koala, be the koala. "I'm intervening the only way I know how!" I shouted right back.

"With what?" He spun around. "Scaring the shit out of me and choking me to death? Claws. Please. Damn it, Abs, your nails are sharp. I swear to all that's holy, if you move your heel down, I will murder you and feel zero guilt!"

I moved my heel down, hitting him in the dick just hard enough to notice that he was..er…hard.

Really?

Violence did it for him?

I moved my heel again.

He froze.

I froze.

His chest rose and fell as he stood, me on his back, him staring at the wall.

I didn't know what to do.

Again, I just went with it and very slowly crawled my way to his front. He let me. He allowed me to wrap myself around him and grab hold. He gripped my thighs almost painfully as he stared me down, his towel barely holding on. Then again, so was my sanity.

His eyes had always been so blue, so easy to get lost in.

"What could you possibly need that's so important that you mauled me like a cheetah from the zoo?" he said in a hoarse voice. "Real adults just say 'hey, what's up?' or maybe even, 'I have a question,'" he said slowly. "And yet you pounced like I was the zebra and you were the lion. Which, let's be honest, is kind of perfect, all things considered."

I put my hand over his mouth, still holding on with one hand while he held me elevated, pressed against every hot inch of him. How was he not affected? I had clothes on, and I was ready to rub against him until we both screamed in ecstasy.

His eyebrows shot up as if to say, "*Really? And now I'm not allowed to talk?*"

"I can't do this, the silent treatment. I can't," I said in a hoarse voice. "Yes, I want to talk to you. Yes, we need to talk. But you can't keep ignoring me if that's going to happen." I moved my hand.

"Actually, I can." He gritted his teeth. "I'm not ready."

And just like that, moved his hands. I would have fallen on my ass had I not seen the look in his eyes and pulled my feet away from his hips.

Suddenly enraged, I charged after him.

He didn't see me coming as I tackled him to the floor. "We are going to talk about this. Now!"

"Are you serious right now?" He batted my hands away. I pulled his towel. He was naked, but I wasn't giving it back. "Give me my towel back!"

"It's a washcloth!"

"It's a towel!"

"It's an inch long."

He made a face. "If it was an inch long, I'd look like I was hung like a horse. It's at least twelve inches."

"The dishcloth or your dick?"

"You would know!" he roared.

I moved to smack him in the face. He grabbed my hands and shoved me away, flipping me onto my back and straddling me. I couldn't help but look. He was so well made. I mean, really. All lean muscle and giant...I gulped. Parts.

The first time we'd had sex, I'd asked if he would rip me in two.

He'd actually looked it up because my concern was warranted. The guy was perfect. Why did I always make things worse?

He pinned my wrists to the floor and moved over me. His dark, wet hair fell over his forehead. "This isn't how we solve this."

"No," I whispered. "It isn't."

His eyes fell to my mouth, and before I thought about it, I leaned up with every ounce of strength I had and kissed him.

I was more than shocked when he kissed me back, when his mouth moved so hungrily across my lips that I finally understood the meaning of being devoured during a kiss.

His mouth opened as if he were trying to decide if he wanted to scream, bite me, or just keep kissing. My hands moved to his shoulders and wrapped around his neck as I pulled him down hard against me, sliding my body against his. I could feel the dampness of the towel against the skin on my thighs, and my jean shorts hiked up as he ran his hands up my ass.

Our teeth clacked together as he angled his head and then reached for my shirt to pull it off.

This was happening.

But I had no idea what it was.

I was in Ty Cuban's arms.

I was angry.

He was furious.

It was our moment.

One I couldn't turn away from because this moment had been ten years in the making. And as rough and aggressive as it was, as angry as it felt, it was us.

He rolled his hips against me and then moved his mouth down my neck, biting below my ear before whispering, "I still hate you."

My laugh came out loud, my voice gritty. "Ditto."

His lips met mine again. His tongue tasted like orange juice. I'd never been so thirsty in my entire life as I tried to kiss him harder, ignoring the sting of tears as my heart hammered against my chest as if to remind me that I was his, I'd always only ever been his.

"Yes," I said against his mouth when my bra went flying. "Please," I begged when his hands pulled my shorts all the way down.

He slapped my bare ass. "Can't complain about no underwear." It was a mumble against my mouth, but it felt like he was already inside me. He was barely touching me, but his hands were massive. Every inch of my skin screamed out for him, for more attention as I felt his length pulse against my thigh. That was for me. Me.

He hesitated.

I didn't want him to.

I knew this wouldn't fix what was broken.

But I was done thinking.

Done arguing.

He pulled away. Our eyes searched each other, maybe for permission for this ceasefire or whatever it was. The silence was filled with deep breaths, apologies, words that neither of us wanted to say. I ran my hands through his thick hair, and he let out a curse.

Still looking at me, his eyes wide open.

Both of our eyes open.

He pressed into me.

I sucked in a sharp breath at the initial feel of him, and my thighs shook as I tried to relax. And then he pulled back. "What do you want, crazy girl?"

With tears in my eyes, I whispered, "Us."

He pushed all the way in and murmured against my mouth, "Good answer."

"I'm not crazy." I bit his bottom lip, earning a dark chuckle.

"Yeah, okay." His movements were slow, purposeful. I couldn't hold back the sounds coming from my mouth, the words that basically praised him for being a sex god. At least I didn't tell him that we should build a shrine.

That would be weird.

Everything about Ty was long, fluid, his movements wave-like, nothing rushed. Every moment was stretched out until I thought I might die if he didn't move faster, harder. I gripped his biceps, earning another deep kiss as he panted against my neck

"More," I encouraged. "Please, Ty, I need more of you."

"Literally impossible," he breathed as he gripped my ass and drove into me harder, just the way I needed him to. I sucked in a sharp breath at the feel of him being so deep, us so connected. I never wanted to let the moment go. I wished we could stay on that floor forever.

"This"—he pinched my ass and then cupped it with his hand, moving his fingers lower between my thighs, driving me insane—"is"— I thought he was going to say "*mine.*" Instead, he cursed like he couldn't say the words, was afraid of what they meant.

A knock sounded on the door at about the exact moment I felt my body find its release. He growled against my mouth, his kiss painful as he followed. The knock got louder.

He was still inside me, both of us panting, when the familiar voice came. "Seriously, Ty, open the hell up."

It was Drew.

Ty quickly jumped to his feet. "One minute."

Panicked, I looked around for my clothes then dove on the other side of the couch when Ty strutted past me in his sweatpants and opened the door a crack. "'Sup?"

I rolled my eyes. He could at least try to sound normal.

Drew didn't even blink or tease or do anything.

It was complete silence followed by a, "I'm sorry, man, it was an accident. There was nothing they could do. She didn't make it."

What?

I pulled my shirt on over my head, grabbed my shorts, and then made my way toward the door.

Drew did a double-take while Ty slowly slid down the door and onto the floor, his head in his hands.

My heart cracked. "What's going on?"

"His aunt got in a crash. She didn't make it. I've been calling, but his phone's on silent I think, and…" Tears pricked my eyes. "I know they weren't close, but she was the only family he had…"

He didn't say "*left*," but we both knew it.

Drew looked ready to call someone, ready to rally the guys.

But that's not what Ty needed.

No, the only thing Ty had ever needed was to feel like he hadn't been abandoned by everyone he loved.

The only thing Ty needed was acceptance, love, a family—something stable.

I gave Drew a knowing look. "I'm here. I have this."

His nostrils flared. I could tell he wanted to say something or maybe argue, so I reached out and touched Drew's shoulder, while Ty sat motionless in the doorway.

"Okay." Drew sighed. "Call me?"

"Yeah." I watched him walk away and then joined Ty on the floor.

He didn't look at me.

Sadness poured out of me as I slowly crawled across the small space between us, then cupped his face with my hands. "It's going to be okay."

"I have no one."

My heart dropped to my stomach, then the final few pieces that still hadn't broken after our relationship shattered.

They were his, all those pieces. No matter how many times I tried to keep them safe, they had always been his.

I wrapped my arms around his neck and whispered against his skin, "You have me. You will always have me. No matter what."

He squeezed me tight.

And I prayed that I was right. That everything really would be okay.

Chapter Fourteen

Ty

Somehow, my legs carried me into the bedroom. Either that or Abigail had been lifting weights as if preparing for this very moment where she'd have to carry my pathetic body somewhere safe.

The bed didn't feel like my own. I didn't know why that was what I chose to fixate on, but the sheets smelled like her.

I lay on my stomach, or maybe she just shoved me face-down. Either way, I was tempted to put the pillow over my head and ask her to leave.

That was, until she started rubbing my back in slow circles.

Funny how something so simple could be a trigger for me. I mean, a back rub? But it was the only thing I remembered from my mom.

The fact that she used to rub my back when I was sleeping. I was too young to remember a lot of things, but I remembered that. When I went to go live with my aunt, I remembered asking her for circles.

She'd thought I meant actual circles and drew me a circle then left the room.

I didn't know what it meant to have circles on your back, so I'd started crying and pointing to my back as best as I could, asking for circles on my back.

She'd taken me to the doctor and told him that my parents' deaths were making me crazy.

She'd never once asked me to explain, and when I tried to, she left the room like she couldn't be bothered, as if my existence irritated her.

I'd never forget the look the doctor gave me. His ruddy face paled, and for the first time since my parents' deaths, someone pulled me into their lap, held me close, and rubbed my back.

He'd told me to be strong.

He'd told me I was a big boy.

He rubbed my back.

I squeezed my eyes shut as a tear slipped. I hated this feeling of weakness, this sense of abandonment. Because even though there was no love lost with my aunt, she was still the only family I had left.

She was still the person who'd helped raise me as best she could. She'd never wanted kids, everything was about her career, so it was either me or her high-paying job.

And she'd begrudgingly chosen me because she loved her sister.

I think the worst part was that they looked alike. I remembered being so deliriously sick with a fever that I thought my mom had come back as an angel.

It was my aunt.

It was the first time I'd seen her cry. When I reached for her and said, "Mama."

Abigail's hand moved over my skin, and then she lay down next to me, making me the small spoon as she held me.

I didn't realize I was crying so hard until the pillow felt wet.

I hated crying.

I'd never in my adult life cried in front of another person— especially one who could use that weakness against me.

Bad timing, universe.

Bad freaking timing.

Give me something I'd wanted for ten damn years and then take away the one thing I'd always needed as penance.

Family.

I grunted out a curse and flipped onto my back, nearly colliding with Abigail as I crossed my arms and stared up at the boring, white ceiling. Dead. She was dead. There would be funeral arrangements, things I needed to take care of, pay for, not to mention the press release.

The media was going to be all over it, weren't they?

I wasn't in the right state of mind to talk to them—to talk to anyone.

My grief quickly morphed into horror as the last few months of my life came crashing down around me.

The Grammys, the music camp, Abigail, and my aunt.

I'd always known that choices decided your journey and you couldn't blame anyone but yourself. But in this instance, I just felt trapped by the consequences of my choices, hers, and the universe's very real anger at me.

"I know you guys weren't close," Abigail said in a raspy voice. "But I also know that it didn't matter. She was still your family…"

"Yeah." I found my voice. "I don't want to talk about it."

"I know." She put her hand on my chest and sat up, her eyes locking with mine. "Maybe you should take a few days, grieve…"

"Take a few days," I repeated. "Grieve." I snorted out a laugh and shot to my feet. "You know what the worst part about all of this is?"

Her eyes widened at my sudden movement as she crawled across the bed and stood in front of me. "What?"

"You," I sneered. "You're the worst part. Because I look at you and I remember what it feels like to really hurt, to really lose. Shit, you were my family, Abs, and I lost you. You walked away from me. A person doesn't just get over that. The only family I had left is dead, and all I keep thinking about is the fact that it hurt worse seeing you walk away."

Abigail's eyes filled with tears. "I'm so—"

"Don't." I held up my hand. "Don't say you're sorry. I don't want to hear it, not right now…" I felt the sadness then, creeping up my throat, clawing at my skin, begging to be set free. I wanted to blame her, when I knew it took two. When I knew we'd both messed up. "My aunt's dead."

Her face fell. "I know, Ty."

"She's never coming back, just like my parents." My voice shook as I glared at her. "Just like you."

I didn't give her a chance to argue, I just left the room and grabbed my keys.

"Ty, wait!" She chased after me.

"I need air." I didn't look back, just hopped into my rental and drove off toward the direction of the boardwalk—toward the studio.

Chapter Fifteen

Abigail

I wanted to chase after him, but I wasn't sure if it would help or hinder what he was going through. I felt like the worst sort of person. I honestly didn't even want to look in the mirror. My chest hurt for him, my body was sore from him—just like my heart.

I quickly opened my group text and asked for help.

Me: *Hey, guys, Ty just took off, he's really struggling. Not sure if Drew told everyone, but his aunt was killed in a car accident. I tried to help. He was upset and drove off.*

Drew: *Thought you had it handled.*

Me: *This isn't the time, Drew, or I will murder you.*

Zane: *She knows Krav Maga, just saying…and Seaside is small. We'll find him. Let's just hope it's not in a drug and alcohol-induced stupor.*

Drew: *Shit.*

Will: *I'll make some calls about the funeral arrangements and make sure everything is taken care of, all right?*

I breathed a sigh of relief.

Me: *Thanks.*

Trevor: *I told him to write some sad songs, maybe he's at the studio?*

Alec: *I'll meet you there.*

Demetri: *Already on my way.*

Lincoln: *Hey, guys, just catching up. Jaymeson and I are together and just read all the texts. We'll let his publicity team know they need to prepare a statement. Hey,*

Will, send us one of his recent shots at the Grammys.

Will: *Already sent over.*

As I read the texts, all I kept thinking was that Ty was one hundred percent wrong.

His family wasn't dead.

It was right the hell here.

In this text conversation.

With these guys.

They would bleed for him, die for him, do whatever it took to make sure he was okay.

I swiped my palm across my wet cheek.

Me: *I don't know what he would do without you guys, thank you. I'm going to try to make myself useful around here…*

Zane: *Food. Lots and lots of food.*

Drew: *There's a reason people bring food after a funeral. If you're eating, you're not thinking about your heart breaking.*

Me: *What if you're the reason his heart is breaking? What if he's projecting all of the past present and future feelings on you? Pretty sure a casserole doesn't work…*

Alec: *It would for me.*

Demetri: *That's because Nat can't cook.*

Alec: *I'll go ahead and let her know to cancel that pumpkin bread order.*

Demetri: *HOW DARE YOU? WE MADE A PACT! I meant COOKING, not baking, you dumbass…oh, and remind her extra chocolate chips.*

Zane: *How do I get in on this bread business?*

Demetri: *You have to be her favorite so…never.*

Zane: *I'm everyone's favorite.*

Trevor: *lolololol Oh, sorry, I meant to say that in my head.*

Me: *Guys? Hello?*

Drew: *I was hesitant to even respond because it looks like you were making him feel just fine when I stopped by to deliver the bad news…*

Zane: *Tell us everything.*

Will: *What did you do?*

Trevor: *Son of a bitch, Abigail, tell me it's not true.*

Will: *We need to do damage control.*

Alec: *This is bad.*

Demetri: *You couldn't just NOT touch him? I know he has a nice body, but.*

Zane: *It's nice I guess…but I mean, if you're comparing…*

Me: *You guys aren't helping my anxiety levels, and before you start pointing your fingers, remember, it takes two.*

Alec: *Unless you're Demetri and lazy as hell.*

Demetri: *No complaints last night.*

Drew: *Look, all I'm saying is it looked like you guys had just been naked, his pants were barely on, your shirt looked inside out, your lipstick was smudged, and your hair had seen better days…*

Guilt slammed into me.

Me: *We had sex.*

Will: *WHAT THE HELL WERE YOU THINKING?*

Drew: *She wasn't. Obviously.*

Trevor: *He can't go through that again, we can't…our band won't survive…*

Tears stung my eyes.

Me: *Please, just for once, listen. We were on the same page and…I want to try with him. I miss him. I know he misses me. He just…he's having a hard time forgiving right now, and we were just getting ready to talk things out when the doorbell rang.*

Trevor: *Found him. He's at the studio.*

Demetri: *Yeah…he looks…*

Alec: *Shit.*

Me: *Guys? GUYS! Is he okay? What's wrong? Is he safe?*

Drew: *Just got here, I'll text you later, Abs. He's…safe.*

What the hell did that even mean? He was safe, but he was high out of his mind? He was safe but bleeding? He was safe but he'd gotten wasted in the last fifteen minutes?

Panic hit me so hard I had no choice but to do exactly what the guys had suggested.

I baked.

Chapter Sixteen

Ty

The studio was dark, lessons were done for the day, obviously, and the sun was going down. I was alone.

Just me, the guitar, a soundboard, and several instruments that I knew how to play but refused to even touch.

She was dead.

The woman who'd raised me as best she could.

I pulled out my phone. I had a dozen texts and several missed calls from Abigail, but I couldn't bring myself to call or text back.

I couldn't sit in that bedroom with her, seeing the look on her face, wondering if she was comforting me because it was convenient, she felt sorry for me, or because she still loved me.

And I hated that on the day I found out about my aunt's death, the one thing that kept circulating in my mind was whether it could work. Could Abs feel the way about me that I felt about her?

Could she be mine?

I picked up one of Trevor's acoustic guitars and started strumming from my spot on the stool. The sound booth wasn't recording, I was just strumming, and then a few words came out.

They sounded funny, probably because lyrics were supposed to float in the air right along the waves of the music—and these felt too heavy to stay there long. They seemed like the sort of words that soared and then crashed to the ground, only to repeat the process.

Darkness built inside me as I strummed harder and harder. "You were never mine to begin with, my heart was never yours to break. It was my first stumble, our first mistake, lying to ourselves that you were mine to take."

The light in the booth turned green. I glanced up, still strumming, to see Trevor walk in on the other side of the glass. His hands moved to the soundboard, and then the door opened. Demetri, Zane, Alec, and Drew all walked in. One grabbed drumsticks, the other snagged the bass, still another the electric, and finally, Zane sat at the piano.

They all looked at me with expectant faces because we were one and the same, weren't we? Musicians felt too much. And when we did, we had to use music to communicate because simple words never matched superior emotions, did they? Like puzzle pieces that didn't fit. Our emotions needed something bigger, something more complex in order to straighten themselves out, to find their place.

I strummed my guitar and nodded at Trevor.

And just like that, we were recording my pain.

I finally felt a little bit of the ache in my chest ease.

Hours later, it was close to midnight, and I left that studio feeling better than when I'd walked in.

I stopped outside and looked up. It was a clear night, the first one we'd had in Seaside since I arrived.

Of course it would be today.

"Hey." Drew jogged up to me. "We need to talk."

Dread crept over me. "Does it need to be now?"

"Yes." His eyes flashed. "Right now."

"Fine." I kicked at the dirt and started walking. He fell into step beside me as we made our way down the boardwalk and onto the sand. I kicked off my sandals and let the cold sand seep through my toes as the sound of the crashing waves filled the air.

Drew did the same thing.

Several bonfires were scattered around the beach, and laughter fought with the sound of the tumultuous waves.

I stopped a few hundred feet before the wet sand and sat down, pulling my knees to my chest. "So, what's up?"

"How are you doing? I mean, really?" Drew's voice was quiet, like a whisper.

"What would you do?" I turned to look at him.

Drew looked confused. "If someone I loved died?"

"No. If the person you loved most in the world walked out of your life then came stomping back in like a bull in a china shop, all angry and beautiful. What would you do?"

"She did." Drew cursed under his breath. "Only she didn't want me. She wanted someone else."

"Was it your fault?"

Drew was quiet and then said, "Yeah, all of it was my fault—her hurt, my hurt, Will's hurt. If you have to point fingers, and I really wish you wouldn't because you know I haven't dealt with this shit yet, they would all point at me."

"I loved her."

Drew put his arm around me in a bro hug. "No, you *love* her."

"I love her," I admitted as the waves drowned out the sound of my voice. "I just don't know how to love her anymore, how to be an *us* anymore. Every time I think I can, it feels like something happens."

"My opinion?"

"Get drunk off my ass and spiral?" I offered.

He burst out laughing. "Yeah, no. That's a horrible idea, especially if you want to get her back. Though nobody would blame you. I just don't want you going to that place again, it's not a very fun one..."

"No." I shuddered.

"Go home, talk to her, hash it out. And if after all that yelling and kissing, you still feel like you'd rather fight with her than walk away for good, you have your answer."

I tilted my head. "That's...not a typical Drew response."

"I'm sober, so..." He shrugged.

I laughed again. "Right."

"Those tracks were good...you write well from your pain." Drew stood and offered me his hand. "But I have a question. That deep, dark place you were writing from, it's where your relationship with Abigail exists. I know you cared for your aunt, I know she was all you had, but I also know that if you guys try to make this work and Abigail walks away forever—I just...I don't know if you can survive that hit. You're a strong man, Ty, but speaking from personal experience, from hating life every single day because you see yourself with someone who doesn't want to be with you, who can't be with you? I wouldn't wish that on anyone, not even my worst enemy."

"Ouch." I hung my head, noting the sadness in his eyes, recognizing the anger that lurked beneath that very intense look.

I wore that same expression every day.

"Yeah, well." Drew slapped me on the back. "The truth hurts."

"At least we can feel it now that we aren't high," I pointed out.

He burst out laughing. "Yeah, give me pain any day. It means I'm alive and not some washed-up rock star shooting up."

"Amen," I grumbled as we walked back toward the lights of the boardwalk and past the bonfires and laughing people who I knew were probably taking pics of us.

We were used to it.

And for the first time in a very long while, my attention wasn't focused on my fans. It was focused on the girl waiting for me, the one that got away, the woman I still loved and had never been able to let go.

Chapter Seventeen

Abigail

I made a feast.

Started with chocolate chip cookies, moved right on to a homemade chocolate cake, and then wondered if everything was too dark and chocolatey, so I looked on Pinterest for a few other fun recipe ideas. I totally messed them up and settled for Rice Krispie treats.

My nemesis.

How can you only eat just one?

I made two batches just in case and then sat and waited. It had been hours since he left. At least I knew he was safe. I just wasn't sure what version of Ty I would get when he came back to the condo, and I had to be up early for the camp in the morning.

I was just nodding off when I heard the door open. I shot to my feet, the blanket pooling by my toes as I waited for Ty to make his way in.

I expected him to be sad, maybe drunk, prayed he wouldn't be high and that this hadn't pushed him over the edge like it so easily could. If anything, he looked calm. Relaxed. Why was I the one that was a wreck?

"Smells good." He let out a little grunt then moaned when he saw the Rice Krispie treats. The insane man picked the entire pan up and joined me on the couch.

I frowned. "You realize that you're supposed to cut it into pieces?"

"The way I see it"—he started very carefully pulling the sticky substance from the pan—"is it's one giant square. Technically, this is one Rice Krispie treat. Why would I cut it up?"

I narrowed my eyes. "I can't argue with that logic."

"Thank God there's food," he said between bites and then turned to me, mouth full. "Sorry, want some?"

I almost hit the pan out of his hands. See? This is why we never worked, he hit on my every last nerve! I had been worried sick about him, and now he was just sitting on the couch eating dessert like it wasn't a big deal.

He was mid-chew when it happened. When the spark ignited in my soul. "I was worried!"

I didn't whisper it. I shouted it.

I needed to learn control or anger management. I just couldn't find any other way to communicate with him.

"I know." He swallowed and put the pan down.

"I texted everyone. I had no idea where you were, if you were okay. If you were...you know." I felt the hot tears threaten to escape. "I—"

He cupped my cheek. "I know you were worried. I just needed some space. I needed to think, and I tend to not think when I'm with you. I just say whatever's on my mind..."

"Same," I huffed. "I don't mean to, it's like I can't control it."

"We've always been that way, why would now be any different?" His hand dropped.

"We're older for one thing," I pointed out. "And I should do better to control the rage I feel."

"It's not rage, it's fear," he said quietly. "And I know exactly what that feels like. I face it every day, this anger that I want to keep wrapped up around me so that every time you say something or do something, it hits the shield instead of my still-broken heart."

I sucked in a sharp breath. "Ty—"

"No, let me say this. I need to say it, and then you need to go to bed."

"Don't be bossy," I muttered.

The corner of his mouth lifted in a sexy smile. "A tiger can't just change its spots."

I rolled my eyes. "Stripes."

"Are you correcting me?"

"Yes."

"Just can't help herself..." he said, more to himself than me, and then looked my way. "Today was a mistake."

Not what I'd expected him to say.

My world stopped while I stared at him, waiting for him to say, "*just kidding*," or explain.

A few heartbeats later, he grabbed my hands and brought them to his mouth. "We have no business hooking up if that's all it's going to be, Abs. Because I'll always want more, and I don't know if you're capable of giving it to me or if you just aren't willing. Either way, I'm not a summer fling, and neither are you. You're better than that. So, unless we get this shit figured out between us, we can't..."

I felt myself deflate. He wanted more. We both did. I just didn't know how to go about it.

"Okay." I took a deep breath. "So, we abandon the physical and just focus on...friendship?" I almost winced at the hungry look on his face.

He quickly recovered and stood. "Yup, friendship. My favorite thing in the world...being best friends with a girl whose boobs I used to trace with my tongue. Good times."

I threw a pillow at his chest and stood. "You're right, you know?"

"What's that?" He cupped his ear. "Did you just say I was right?"

"I can see the headlines now. *Ty Cuban found dead from suffocation.*" I held the pillow high.

He ripped it out of my hands. "And below that, it would say...*and haunts Von Abigail forever.*"

I leaned up and kissed him on his cheek. "Joke's on you...he already does."

He reached out and grabbed my hips, holding me close to him. I could feel the burn of his fingertips.

We were kindling waiting to be lit.

A match that refused to be blown out.

We were fireworks and chaos all mixed into one.

He swallowed, his eyes lingering on my mouth before he slowly stepped away. "You should go to bed."

"Only if you sleep, too."

"Afraid I'm going to leave again?"

"Yes," I said honestly. "I am."

His face fell. "I'm sad, not suicidal."

"Yeah, but I didn't know that, Ty. So, please just…communicate better so I don't bake you a seven-tier cake next time, all right?"

His smile was wide. "Does this cake have extra frosting?"

"Be serious!"

"I am!" he roared. "I like frosting! Can it be blue?"

"Oh God, this is what I have to look forward to for the rest of the summer, isn't it?"

He picked me up off my feet and twirled me around then sat me down and pointed me toward my room. Then he slapped my ass and chuckled. "Buckle up, Abs, you know I like wild rides."

My cheeks heated like fire the entire way to my room, and when I shut my door, I nearly combusted.

Living with him would be fine, totally fine. Not jumping him…even easier. I'd lasted ten years, what were a few more weeks? Months? Being his friend again, establishing trust, hmm…

Nothing. I would be fine.

Totally. Fine.

Chapter Eighteen

Ty

Captain's log. Summer guitar lessons, week six. I can barely walk into the room without seriously injuring my dick. It feels like years. My body wants what it wants, and it wants Abigail—painfully.

She touched me today—by accident. Then again, it wasn't like I was making it easy on her. I was too hard for that. Ha, see what I did there? Our friendship was growing. It was all sunshine and ponies, blah, blah, blah—I almost died from that touch.

Her fingers were cold. You'd think my dick would be like…"*Nope, not happening, warm those bad boys up and then we can talk.*" Instead, it was so desperate for attention that I could have sworn I felt my entire being flinch toward her in an effort to draw more attention to the zipper of my jeans.

I clenched my teeth.

She apologized and asked if I wanted syrup.

Like that was helpful.

Images of syrup filling my hands, spilling over her breasts like a waterfall into my mouth filled my mind so hard and fast that I stared at her for a solid two minutes before she asked if I'd had a stroke.

Yeah, she'd said stroke.

I just groaned and nearly jumped off the balcony to put myself out of my misery.

We still fought.

But it was more over the remote control and who got the last taco on Taco Tuesday. We'd fallen into a routine that I never wanted to walk away from, even if I did have to see her tampons scattered around the bathroom.

And, yeah, I may have pissed her off a few times, like a dozen, and earned the bed full of feminine products I got. But I just told her she was hormonal.

The next day, I could have sworn Satan took hold of her body as she launched herself over me just to grab the Hershey bar out of my hands.

I had legit scratches.

She never apologized.

I had to get friggin' Band-Aids.

Six weeks seemed like a long time...and that was because it was. Especially when you loved someone. When you truly wanted to be a part of them in every way, and when you were the one that'd said you needed space.

Part of the reason was because I needed time to focus on my aunt's funeral and everything that meant. Thankfully, the guys were all there when I needed them and helped me, down to flying out with me over a forty-eight-hour period for the service.

Abs even came.

The private jet was not big enough for the two of us. Within ten minutes of taking off, we were fighting again, this time over a cookie. Drew announced that if we didn't have sex, he was going to have a nervous breakdown from all the sexual tension.

He wasn't wrong.

And every other guy had a girl to go home to.

Except Drew.

Whoops.

And now? Now, I was on week six with Connor, thankful that I had one of my favorite students to take my mind off Abigail.

He was my last lesson of the day.

He walked in with a sullen expression on his face and then pulled out his chair and plopped into it.

"Something wrong?" I picked up my guitar.

"No." He kicked my chair.

Yeah, right. "You sure? Oh shit, man, you going through puberty?"

He scowled, making me burst into laughter.

After a few more minutes of him looking grumpier than I felt, which was a hell of a lot of grumpiness in one room, I put my guitar down. "Look, I'd like to think we're friends, right? Tell me what it is, and maybe I can help you. Is it your mom?"

"No."

"Is it me?"

"No."

"Duh, because I'm awesome. So, what is it?"

"It's Caroline."

"The song?"

"The girl!" He threw up his arms. "I like her, okay? She's doing the summer camp, and my mom couldn't afford to let me do every day, just a few days a week since I'm taking guitar lessons from Trevor. And there's this kid, Jonas."

"The plot thickens." I grinned. "Go on."

"So, Jonas is super popular, but he's a total jerk, and he brought her candy when I wasn't there, and now people are saying she likes Jonas more."

"I don't like Jonas."

"Jonas sucks," he agreed.

"Does Jonas even have game?"

"His parents own a taffy store."

"Well, sh—I mean, crap."

"You can say shit. Mom says that when she sees spiders."

"Her and me both," I joked and then sobered. "All right, I say we come up with a grand gesture for Caroline."

"What's that?" Connor's interest looked piqued.

"Dude! It's what every awesome movie has! I mean, think Aquaman. He got the trident and became king, and what did he get out of it?"

"Umm, a kingdom?"

"A GIRL!" I all but shouted. "And not just any girl, a princess."

Connor's face lit up. "Yeah, I guess he did!"

"Grand gesture."

"Except, I'm not Aquaman."

"No, bro, you're better because you're a musician. Trust me on this. A good voice, good talent, trumps all those muscles any day." Sadly, not true, but meh...we'd work on the scrawny body later. Kid had time, after all.

He licked his lips and then slowly nodded. "Okay, so I have to do something cool."

"Something beyond cool," I agreed and then grinned. "It's open mic night tonight."

"So?"

"So, it's open mic night," I repeated. "And I have a fool-proof plan. You just make sure Caroline is there and that the little crapface Jonas sees you win her over."

He burst out laughing. "Yeah, I can send her a text. Just gotta ask my mom to do it on her phone since she won't let me have a texting plan."

Gee, I wonder why? I smiled as he pulled out his phone and called his mom, then asked if she could send a text for him.

Coolest kid ever.

Maybe I should steal him? Save the whole baby poop phase and just have a little badass?

Kidding.

Maybe.

Kidnapping was a crime so...I'd just stay the cool mentor. But really, it made me think about things that friends didn't think about.

Like Abigail pregnant with our son or daughter.

Like us settling down after the tour was done.

Putting down roots.

Me wrapping her in my arms and making her coffee in the morning, touching her swelling belly, feeling kicks.

"All right!" Connor interrupted my daydreaming. "Mom's gonna do it. Now we have to plan something cool. Got any ideas?"

"Bro." I put my hand on his shoulder. "Strap in, because we're getting you a girlfriend."

"Not that I need help, though." He sniffed.

"Right. I mean, you've got this. But why not use me, you know?"

"Right," he agreed quickly.

"Grab your guitar," I instructed. "I'm going to teach you the song *Sweet Caroline*."

Chapter Nineteen

Abigail

If living without Ty Cuban for ten years was heartbreaking, then living with him was absolute torture. The man needed more clothes. I had half a mind to burn what tight jeans he did have and toss out all the shirts that showed off his impressive body way too often. He ate like a horse, it wasn't fair.

And if I had to see him walk to the fridge and chug orange juice in nothing but that sorry excuse for a towel one more time, I would not be held responsible for my actions.

I clenched my teeth.

Today was open mic, which meant I was up with the band, helping the kids with their songs, when all I really wanted was to just see Ty. We'd fallen into this easy friendship where we refused to touch one another unless we were fighting—which was often.

So the whole no-touch rule really didn't work with people as explosive as us. If I wasn't walking by him and tripping him or hitting him in the back of the head, he was stealing my pillow, blankets, or shoving me out of the way and winking.

See? Torture!

At least we were getting along.

We were together.

I swallowed the lump in my throat. Together. Just not the way I wanted to be. I wanted more, needed it more than I could even process logically.

How had I ever walked away that first time? You couldn't pay me to turn my back on him now.

Maybe it was the years of maturity.

Maybe it was knowing the truth about myself, the reality that I'd been young, stupid, afraid, and judging one mistake as if I were perfect.

I wasn't.

Far from it.

"All right," Zane said into the microphone. "We have one last late entry before you guys are excused for the day."

I tapped my iPad and grinned. I loved playing *Sweet Caroline*, but what was better was that I saw Connor's name next to it.

Good for him.

Kids started clapping as Connor made his way towards the stage, with Ty following him.

I gaped as Ty winked at me, slung his guitar over his shoulder, and made his way toward the microphone. "I begged this guy to let me help him with the background vocals."

The kids started laughing.

"Is the house band ready?" Ty turned to me and the rest of the crew. Demetri counted us off while Alec grabbed his electric.

And then Connor grabbed the microphone like a pro and said, "This is for you, Caroline."

I almost died, I was smiling so hard.

Ty strummed out the first few chords. Connor did a good job of following, and then little man was on the microphone starting off the first few bars. "Where it began, I can't begin to know."

The kid had good vocals, I had to admit that.

Ty harmonized with him.

The lyrics affected me, mainly because Ty kept looking at me while he sang. Hands touching hands, touching me, touching you. Oh, sweet God, I was going to combust on stage. He licked his lips and bit down.

I imagined that bite on my body in front of a ton of kids.

I was going to hell.

Connor swung his guitar behind him and grabbed the microphone like a rock star in the making and belted, "Sweet Caroline!"

We all joined in, laughing.

The kids jumped to their feet.

And the girl, the one who must have been Caroline, was shoved forward by her friends. Her eyes were wide, her smile even wider, and she started singing with him, and then all the kids were waving their hands in the air.

Ty kept playing while Connor sang his heart out. Alec, Demetri, and Zane looked so into it that I wondered if the song would ever end.

And then Connor turned around, pulled off his shirt, and on his little painted chest were the words *Caroline, be mine.*

I laughed until I had tears, and then Ty set down his guitar while Connor sang the last few words and did the exact same thing.

I was flashed by tight abs, and then in the same writing, I saw, *Von Abigail, be mine too?*

I stopped playing.

Would have dropped my guitar had it not been strapped.

Kids cheered.

The song ended, and all of Connor's friends ran to the stage to pat him on the back. Finally, Caroline hugged him.

I had tears.

Maybe for her.

Perhaps for me.

Ty started walking toward me—swaggering was more like it—and then he tilted my chin toward him and whispered, "What do you say?"

"I say I was going to take advantage of you tonight and chase you around until you said yes, so...good timing."

I swallowed his laugh with a kiss, throwing my arms around his neck as he deepened it in front of all the kids, only to pull back and give Connor a high-five.

"See? Told ya it would work. Music transcends."

I looked between them, choking on the emotion of how Ty was with Connor, how good of a dad he would be. I nearly lost it again. "Yeah," I croaked. "It really does transcend."

Chapter Twenty

Ty

Abigail had to stay late for a staff meeting, which meant that I went back to the condo in a cloud of sexual frustration and intense irritation. How long did staff meetings even take?

I made myself useful and put in some leftovers from the night before, then went and grabbed her favorite wine and uncorked it.

It still smelled horrible to me, as most alcohol did, but if she wanted it, I was more than happy to provide it.

It had been over an hour, and all I wanted was to tell her that I wanted her. I wanted her more than anything.

It wasn't that it had taken me these last six weeks to realize that.

I'd realized it ten years ago.

Time had never been the issue.

Our maturity was.

The baggage we carried around just got in the way, and I hated that we both made enough mistakes to be guilty of keeping our love away from one another.

I opened the balcony door and went outside to watch the waves. Maybe it wasn't Seaside that I hated, perhaps it was just the rain.

Because in that moment, hearing the crashing of the waves, I felt my body relax in an unreal way.

And then hands wrapped around my middle.

I stiffened and turned. "Meeting done?"

She didn't answer me, just stood up on her tiptoes and pulled me down for a kiss. I wasn't arguing. I kissed her back so hard my mouth would likely be bruised from the pressure. I didn't care. I just needed her taste.

She moaned against my tongue, and then literally kicked out a chair, hopped up onto it without taking her mouth off mine, and jumped into my arms. Her legs wound around my waist.

I laughed against her mouth. "Cool trick, got any more?"

"Guess you'll find out." She rolled her hips against me.

I blacked out. Straight-up forgot my own name and then made quick work of pulling her shirt over her head and tossing it to the floor.

She was wearing a black bralette-looking thing that was all delicate lace. I should probably be a gentleman.

But... Six. Weeks.

I tugged it over her head and tossed it over the balcony, then slammed her back against the wall of the condo, dipping my tongue into her mouth again, tasting her, drinking her in.

She arched and then sank down on my leg, squirming against it.

"Feel good?" I chuckled.

"I've needed you for ten years." She pulled back, her eyes glassy. "I've needed you every single day...and will for the rest of my life."

I swallowed the ball of emotion in my throat. "Promise me it's forever."

"It always was," she said on a sob as tears streamed down her face.

"Yeah." I kissed her, peppered her face with more kisses, then said, "It always was."

"Hey, guys..." Drew's voice sounded. "Not to be a total dick, but I'm feeling triggered...."

"Forgot to tell you. He moved to the condo next door yesterday." I laughed. "Needed some space."

"Space!" he shouted. "Without sexually frustrated musicians!"

"Sorry!" Abigail called.

His eyes rounded as she covered her breasts. I may have preened. Was definitely tempted to hit my chest and be like, "*What? You like what you see? ALL MINE, BRO! MINE!*"

I didn't say that.

But I thought it very aggressively and flipped him off behind her back as I moved us into the house and shut the door.

"So he saw me half-naked," Abigail said on a laugh.

"It probably confused him since it's been so long…" I joked, pulling the curtains tight across the sliding glass door just in case.

When I turned around, all I saw was skin.

Lots and lots of skin.

A few tattoos.

Woman.

My mouth went dry. "So you got out of all your clothes fast."

She lifted a shoulder. "I wanted to save time."

"That's very responsible of you." I took a step toward her and peeled my shirt off my body. Her cheeks flushed bright red. I loved that I still did that to her. I moved to my jeans and then stopped. "Did you want me to go slower?"

"Yes, please, and maybe hum so I have a little bit of dirty music playing while you strip for me?"

"Humming isn't dirty."

She shrugged. "I guess that depends on what you're doing while you hum."

I tripped on my next step, then jerkily pulled down my jeans and tossed them away, rushing toward her and picking her up in my arms. Our kiss was still chaotic, it was still angry, but the anger wasn't directed at each other. It was directed at the fact that it had been too long, and we were the only ones standing in the way, using our hurt as a shield, and our hearts as justification.

"I love you," I said against her lips.

Tears streamed down her face. "And I love you, too."

"Good answer, you can touch my abs now if you want. I know you've been looking," I teased.

She smacked me in all the abs and then kissed my chest. "You should probably make sweet love to me now before I change my mind."

"I like to savor things…" I said honestly. "So, let me savor holding you for a few minutes before I get you all sweaty and mean."

"Mean?"

I chuckled. "You get mean during sex."

"I DO NOT!" she yelled.

I winced. "Right, okay. Of course, you're correct, I'm wrong."

She smacked me. "I just know what I want when I want it."

"A woman who knows her mind…" I leaned down and kissed her

head. "Hot."

"Are you being sarcastic?"

"I wouldn't dream of being sarcastic with you naked in my arms."

She narrowed her eyes then grinned, running her nails down my chest. "You know this means you're stuck with me, right? The loving, the fighting—"

"The cooking, the making up," I finished with a kiss to her neck. "I think I can handle it." I slapped her ass and then picked her up into my arms and walked her into the closest bedroom.

The master.

I tossed her onto the bed and looked my fill, from her hips down her legs, to the tattoos that swirled around her ankle.

"It's love, but it's also part obsession because...damn." I shook my head. "You're like the whole pan."

"Huh?" She laughed. "What?"

"I'm getting there." I crawled over her and could feel the heat of her body, saw the way she bit her swollen bottom lip and waited. Her eyes darted from my mouth to my eyes and then back again. "You're the whole pan of Rice Krispies."

"Ohhh, am I?"

"Yeah." I pressed a kiss to her mouth and whispered, "And you know I don't like sharing..."

She wiggled beneath me. "Then eat your fill..."

"I've been waiting ten years for you to say that." I dug my fingers into her thighs and pulled back. "Sex, and then..." I lowered my head and pressed it against her stomach, away from her face. "You and I are going to play."

"What are you—?"

"Could you not?" I hushed her. "I'm having a moment here, all right?"

"With what?"

"Ah, she wants a demonstration." I moved my fingers down her stomach and teased her the way only a good guitarist should. I mean really. Musician...duh.

She nearly came apart after a few chords. Ha, see what I did there?

"Ty!" She bunched the sheets in her hands. "I really don't think I'll last if you keep doing that."

"This?"

She cursed.

"Or this?" Damn, she was so hot, so ready for me.

"Damn it, Ty!" She squeezed my hands with her thighs. "I need you."

"We'll talk later," I whispered, earning a smack on the back of the head as I returned to her mouth, to her neck, to her perfect breasts.

"This." She sighed happily, and then I was getting forcefully turned and pushed onto my back.

I liked it.

I liked her on top.

I liked watching.

Liked seeing the different emotions that flickered across her face as she touched my skin, as she brazenly grabbed hold of me and put me in my place—quite literally.

"No take-backs, Abs," I whispered.

Her eyes never left mine as she sank onto me. I swore I saw Heaven when she started to move and said, "No take-backs."

This was different than before. Different than any other time. It felt like a promise between two broken hearts as they once again merged together and confessed.

Her head fell back as I ran my hands around her ass and pulled her tighter against me, pumping harder while we got lost in the moment of us.

She shattered in my arms then, that beautiful face making me breathless. And when I followed, when I finally caught my breath, I realized that things were exactly as they should be.

Messy.

Perfect.

Us.

I wouldn't have it any other way.

Chapter Twenty-One

Abigail

We stayed in bed until it was time to get up in the morning. Both of us still had to teach, but I wanted to call in sick so badly.

Ty wasn't any help. Every time I tried to leave the bed, he pulled me back and made me wonder if he was taking some sort of supplement or just making up for lost time. I mean, really, who had sex that much in an eight-hour period?

He did.

We did, apparently.

I had such a big smile on my face that I knew I wouldn't be able to hide it, and since Ty didn't have a student until around noon, he decided to come with me to camp.

"Remember," I said once we got out of the Jeep. "You can't just ask for sexual favors in front of the kids."

He scowled. "I'm not an animal."

I gave him a pointed look just as a few middle-schoolers ran past us laughing.

"Hey, flash me a little boob, just the bottom part," he said in a low whisper.

"Oh, God." I shoved him. "You need therapy."

"Sex is my therapy." His answer. I took a deep breath and tried not to be charmed by his wicked smile and the way he used his hands.

Dear Lord, that man's hands.

Both of them.

I shivered.

He leaned in. "Cold?"

"Shut up," I grumbled.

"Bet I could warm you up."

"If you say one more sexual—"

"I meant with my sweatshirt. Tsk, tsk, get your head out of the gutter. Geez, I'm not an animal for your pleasure and your pleasure alone!"

I sighed. "You done yet?"

"Meh, I got most of it off my chest."

"Good, because we're walking toward children who look up to you. The last thing we need is for one of them to go home and be like, 'Hey, Mom, what's *blowjob* mean?'"

Literally, at that exact second, a kid walked by us, one of my students. He was fourteen.

I would never live this down.

He gave me an embarrassed look and scurried off.

I let out a low growl just as Zane made his way over. "You guys make up?"

I hadn't even noticed Drew until he answered, "All night. My guess, her mouth is swollen, and I saw her boobs."

"Fixate on it some more, why don't you?" Ty snapped.

Drew held out his hands as if he were taking a picture and then shook his head. "Sorry, it's glued in there. If she wasn't one of my best friends, I could give you a run for your money."

"Doubtful." Ty snorted. "I have these."

"Hands? He has hands?" Zane asked, genuine confusion in his voice.

"Put those away!" I hissed.

Zane frowned. "We all have those. They aren't naked. What? He needs gloves?"

I felt myself blush while Ty chuckled. Drew seemed to catch on because he hid his smile behind his own hand.

Alec, Demetri, and Trevor joined us.

"Something funny?" Alec asked.

"She looks happy," Demetri answered. And then a huge gasp. "You guys did it!"

Zane nodded. "Yeah, but she's oddly obsessing about his naked hands."

"Shhhh." I looked around. Most campers were sitting and eating their breakfast while the volunteers went over the day. We were in the staff tent so it wasn't like they could hear us unless they were walking by, but still.

And then Ty, lovable, I-may-kill-him-later Ty, spread his arms wide and said, "My new goal is to get her pregnant."

I put my hands over my flaming face while he received high-fives from everyone all around him.

"Sometimes, it's the worst being the only girl," I grumbled behind my hands.

"Chin up." Zane slapped me on the back. "All the wives will be on tour. The odds will be evened..."

All except Drew.

I didn't say it.

When I looked at him, he was still smiling as if he weren't upset about it. Maybe he was dealing better.

"Speaking of..." Ty cleared his throat and then dropped to his knee.

"Whoa!" Trevor and Drew said it in unison while Zane slowly lifted his phone and started recording with a smile on his face. He would record this.

"Ty." My voice was wobbly. "What are you doing?"

"Exactly what I should have done ten years ago when you tried to walk away...I'm making the grand gesture and proposing, though I may have thrown the other ring out the tour bus window—"

"It came back in and hit Will in the face," Trevor added helpfully. "Even makeup couldn't cover that bruise."

I smiled as fresh tears started slipping down my cheeks.

"Shh, man, he's proposing!" Demetri hit him in the chest.

And then Ty winked. "You're my love. You're my chaos. You're angrier than hell, and I never want to tame you." He knew just what to say, didn't he? Then again, he knew me better than I knew myself. "And even though I threw the other ring out the window and physically injured one of my favorite bandmates—"

Drew cleared his throat.

Ty sighed. "*Second* favorite."

Trevor cleared his throat.

"Shit, guys, I'm proposing here. Fine, my third favorite bandmate."—I laughed—"I did find this in the cereal this morning. Oddly enough, I knew it was time." He held out a tiny ring that had a little sword from an action figure on it. I think it was Marvel. "This is so you know that no matter what happens, I'll fight for you, and you'll fight for me. I swear we'll pick out a ring together, but I refuse to live another second without having you as my fiancée, without knowing you'll be my wife."

I lost it then, grabbed the little plastic ring, shoved it on my finger, and then launched myself into his arms, causing him to fall back against the sand.

He rolled me over. "Is that a yes?"

"It's a hell yes." I kissed him.

"Love you." He cupped my cheeks. "Now..." He sobered. "Kids aren't looking. Just the bottom half, I swear—"

I smacked him on the chest and then threw sand.

He gave me the scary Ty Cuban look, which meant I needed to run. And I did, only to be followed by every single one of them as we made our way to the ocean, laughing, kicking up sand and splashing each other.

Seaside might be my new favorite place.

"Hey, Ty!" I yelled him over. "What about buying a house here?"

His grin was huge. "How 'bout showing me a bit of—?"

"Stop with the boobs, there are children present. I mean, Zane at least counts!"

"Heard that!" Zane yelled.

And then Ty was throwing me over his shoulder and running toward the water, slapping my ass. "I say we get a beach house, at least five bedrooms, for our five children."

I just rolled my eyes and then secretly prayed for exactly that.

"Mrs. Cuban." I sighed dreamily.

"Careful, your girl is showing," Ty warned.

I smacked his ass.

And landed in the water with him standing over me, a gorgeous grin on his face. "I love you."

"I love you, too."

A wave took us both down.

It was the favorite morning of my life.
With my best friend.
My enemy.
The one I'd walked away from.
We were finally together.
Forever.

* * * *

Also from 1001 Dark Nights and Rachel Van Dyken, discover All Stars Fall and Envy.

Sign up for the 1001 Dark Nights Newsletter
and be entered to win a Tiffany Key necklace.

There's a contest every month!

Go to www.1001DarkNights.com to subscribe.

As a bonus, all subscribers can download
FIVE FREE exclusive books!

Discover 1001 Dark Nights Collection Six

Go to www.1001DarkNights.com to subscribe.

QUIET MAN by Kristen Ashley
A Dream Man Novella

ABANDON by Rachel Van Dyken
A Seaside Pictures Novella

THE OPEN DOOR by Laurelin Paige
A Found Duet Novella

CLOSER by Kylie Scott
A Stage Dive Novella

SOMETHING JUST LIKE THIS by Jennifer Probst
A Stay Novella

BLOOD NIGHT by Heather Graham
A Krewe of Hunters Novella

TWIST OF FATE by Jill Shalvis
A Heartbreaker Bay Novella

MORE THAN PLEASURE YOU by Shayla Black
A More Than Words Novella

WONDER WITH ME by Kristen Proby
A With Me In Seattle Novella

THE DARKEST ASSASSIN by Gena Showalter
A Lords of the Underworld Novella

Also from 1001 Dark Nights:
DAMIEN by J. Kenner

Discover More Rachel Van Dyken

All Stars Fall: A Seaside Pictures/Big Sky Novella
By Rachel Van Dyken

She *left*.
Two words I can't really get out of my head.
She left *us*.
Three more words that make it that much worse.
Three being another word I can't seem to wrap my mind around.
Three kids under the age of six, and she left because she missed it. Because her dream had never been to have a family, no, her dream had been to marry a rockstar and live the high life.

Moving my recording studio to Seaside Oregon seems like the best idea in the world right now especially since Seaside Oregon has turned into the place for celebrities to stay and raise families in between touring and producing. It would be lucrative to make the move, but I'm doing it for my kids because they need normal, they deserve normal. And me? Well, I just need a break and help, that too. I need a sitter and fast. Someone who won't flip me off when I ask them to sign an Iron Clad NDA, someone who won't sell our pictures to the press, and most of all? Someone who looks absolutely nothing like my ex-wife.

He's tall.
That was my first instinct when I saw the notorious Trevor Wood, drummer for the rock band Adrenaline, in the local coffee shop. He ordered a tall black coffee which made me smirk, and five minutes later I somehow agreed to interview for a nanny position. I couldn't help it; the smaller one had gum stuck in her hair while the eldest was standing on his feet and asking where babies came from. He looked so pathetic, so damn sexy and pathetic that rather than be star-struck, I took pity. I knew though; I knew the minute I signed that NDA, the minute our fingers brushed and my body became insanely aware of how close he was—I was in dangerous territory, I just didn't know how dangerous until it was too late. Until I fell for the star and realized that no matter how high they are in the sky—they're still human and fall just as hard.

Envy: An Eagle Elite Novella
By Rachel Van Dyken

Every family has rules, the mafia just has more....
Do not speak to the bosses unless spoken to.
Do not make eye contact unless you want to die.
And above all else, do not fall in love.
Renee Cassani's future is set.
Her betrothal is set.
Her life, after nannying for the five families for the summer, is set.
Somebody should have told Vic Colezan that.
He's a man who doesn't take no for an answer.
And he only wants one thing.
Her.
Somebody should have told Renee that her bodyguard needed as much discipline as the kids she was nannying.
Good thing Vic has a firm hand.

Stealing Her

Covet, Book 1
By Rachel Van Dyken
Coming November 5, 2019

From the #1 *New York Times* bestselling author comes an unexpected love story of family, secrets, and the most intimate of deceptions.

My estranged twin brother, Julian, was always the wonder boy—and soon-to-be CEO of our ruthless father's corporation. My mother and me? Left behind. Now, years after tearing our family apart, my father dares to ask *me* for a favor? Pretend to be Julian while he fights to survive a tragic accident. It can save the company. Nobody will be the wiser. It'll be our secret.

I can play Dad's favorite. I'll do it for Julian. And for my mother, who'll want for nothing.

But this double life comes with a beauty of a hitch: my very real feelings for Julian's fiancée, Isobel. Not only am I betraying Julian, I'm deceiving a woman I love. She doesn't suspect a thing. As lies compound, lines are crossed and loyalties tested, all I can ask myself is…what have I done?

Because sooner or later something's got to give. There's no way I'm giving up Isobel. But once the truth is exposed, it might not be my choice at all.

* * * *

We stopped in front of the room.
I swallowed and stared at the metal door.
"Go inside, I'll wait." My dad crossed his arms.
I'd told him I had conditions.
And this was one of them.
I wanted to see him for myself.
I wanted to see that he wasn't dead.
I wanted to tell him I was sorry.
I wanted to ask for his forgiveness.
I wanted to mend all the broken bridges between us.

Most of all I wanted him to know I was doing this for him, for his legacy, for the one thing he wanted the most in this world, the one thing I loathed.

The company.

And even if he woke up hating me, I would walk away knowing I did everything in my power to help him in every way I could.

I took a deep breath and opened the door.

The room smelled like antiseptic.

The lights were low.

And he was hooked up to so many machines my eyes blurred with tears. One machine breathed for him; every second or so it made a noise that had my stomach clenching.

He was alive.

Barely.

His face was covered in bandages, and one of his legs was broken, I knew he had several broken ribs and a collapsed lung going into surgery.

"Hey, Jules." My voice sounded so loud in that room. "You look like shit."

I figured if he could hear me, he would at least smile at that.

"You're also all over the news, which should make you really happy since you love the attention, but that's not why I'm here. Dad came to visit and he said... some things." Shit, how was I even supposed to do this? I cursed and spun around, putting my hands on my head.

"I know how important this job and following in his footsteps is to you, and I guess I just somehow needed you to know that I'm going to work my ass off so that when you wake up, you have everything you've always wanted. I just need you to know that it's not for me, it's for you. I swore I would protect you and I failed. I can't fail in this. I won't," I rasped. "But I really need you to wake up soon because I have no idea what I'm doing, and I have no idea how to do this other than to make it look like you're okay, so that you can have everything you've always wanted." I sighed and then looked at him one last time. "I never stopped loving you. I want you to know that."

I squeezed my eyes shut and hung my head, then turned around and walked back into the hall.

My dad was talking to one of the nurses. She looked at me and I just shook my head. My dad went to great lengths to make everyone think he only had one son, so I was used to that look of confusion. I never told anyone who my father was and didn't even use the Tennyson name. It disgusted me. It represented what my father did to my mom, what he did to Julian, our family.

I took my mom's maiden name and pretended I wasn't a Tennyson.

And my dad let me because he had one son he could control and knew that wasn't me.

Until now.

He looked between me and the nurse and whispered something else, then walked back to me, his swagger so confident I wanted to punch him in the face.

His "only" son was in the ICU fighting for his life, and he was smiling. How the hell was he smiling?

"She won't talk." He adjusted his white silk tie. "The entire ICU's been paid off, and I made a large donation to the hospital this morning. No reporters will be allowed in, nobody knows who you are, remember?"

"I wonder how many people you had to pay off to make that happen," I shot back.

He glared. "I'm offering you a fresh start."

"Right." *Like the fresh start you gave me when you sent me away.* I could feel a headache coming on. "The only reason I'm doing this is for Mom and Julian."

He snorted out a laugh. "You realize your brother hates you."

"And I hate you, so it looks like we're all in good company."

He ignored the comment and started walking, and I knew the expectation was to walk with him so I did.

"All her medical bills," I demanded. "Nobody but the board will know my true identity, and the minute Julian wakes up, he takes over again."

"If he wakes up."

"He'll fucking wake up," I said through clenched teeth.

My dad hesitated like he needed someone to tell him that Julian would fight, and then he agreed, "He's strong. He's a Tennyson."

About Rachel Van Dyken

Rachel Van Dyken is the *New York Times, Wall Street Journal,* and *USA TODAY* Bestselling author of regency and contemporary romances. When she's not writing you can find her drinking coffee at Starbucks and plotting her next book while watching The Bachelor.

She keeps her home in Idaho with her husband and adorable son. She loves to hear from readers!

For more information, visit her website at
http://rachelvandykenauthor.com

Discover 1001 Dark Nights

COLLECTION ONE
FOREVER WICKED by Shayla Black
CRIMSON TWILIGHT by Heather Graham
CAPTURED IN SURRENDER by Liliana Hart
SILENT BITE: A SCANGUARDS WEDDING by Tina Folsom
DUNGEON GAMES by Lexi Blake
AZAGOTH by Larissa Ione
NEED YOU NOW by Lisa Renee Jones
SHOW ME, BABY by Cherise Sinclair
ROPED IN by Lorelei James
TEMPTED BY MIDNIGHT by Lara Adrian
THE FLAME by Christopher Rice
CARESS OF DARKNESS by Julie Kenner

COLLECTION TWO
WICKED WOLF by Carrie Ann Ryan
WHEN IRISH EYES ARE HAUNTING by Heather Graham
EASY WITH YOU by Kristen Proby
MASTER OF FREEDOM by Cherise Sinclair
CARESS OF PLEASURE by Julie Kenner
ADORED by Lexi Blake
HADES by Larissa Ione
RAVAGED by Elisabeth Naughton
DREAM OF YOU by Jennifer L. Armentrout
STRIPPED DOWN by Lorelei James
RAGE/KILLIAN by Alexandra Ivy/Laura Wright
DRAGON KING by Donna Grant
PURE WICKED by Shayla Black
HARD AS STEEL by Laura Kaye
STROKE OF MIDNIGHT by Lara Adrian
ALL HALLOWS EVE by Heather Graham
KISS THE FLAME by Christopher Rice
DARING HER LOVE by Melissa Foster
TEASED by Rebecca Zanetti
THE PROMISE OF SURRENDER by Liliana Hart

On behalf of 1001 Dark Nights,

Liz Berry and M.J. Rose would like to thank ~

Steve Berry
Doug Scofield
Kim Guidroz
Jillian Stein
InkSlinger PR
Dan Slater
Asha Hossain
Chris Graham
Chelle Olson
Kasi Alexander
Jessica Johns
Dylan Stockton
Richard Blake
and Simon Lipskar